A DJ guide and memoir

By Blaze Hunter

Edited by Kevin Hudson

GW00728980

Copyright ©2016 Blaze Hunter

Table of Contents

Foreword by Blaze Hunter

I first met Randy Feelgood in 1980 in a small club in New York called Figaro's, West 56th Street and 7th Avenue. I arrived at the opening night of this refurbished club to witness for myself this legendary performer who, perhaps unintentionally, inspired the whole disco phenomenon to reach out into the mainstream from its humble, underground beginnings as a movement for the few, the oppressed and disenfranchised in the community; the gay, free, blacks and Latinos.

Walking down 56th street I could see police officers holding back the crowds of on-lookers and minor celebrities, straining to see into to the club. There was the usual mixture of the curious, the star struck and the weird and wonderful, all eager for a glimpse of their idols. It was a VIP ticketed event and there was an air of anticipation around New York in the weeks leading up to the big night. Randy Feelgood was back in town.

When I gained entry to the Club, through an inauspicious doorway next to the Rattan Grand Hotel, it was like entering any backstreet bar in the city at that time; a bit tatty with peeling paint on the door frame and two obligatory large gentlemen with afro hair and handle bar moustaches in ill-fitting braided, brushed velvet suits, with a slight bulge under the armpits for their personal firearm. But as I entered, I was instantly assailed by the pulsating rhythm of a driving beat through the small speakers positioned in the main entrance.

I walked the red lamp lit, swirly carpet from the front door and through an 'L' shaped hallway and emerged, seemingly by some invisible magnetic force, in a kaleidoscope of light, sound and colours, bursting around me, onto the epicentre of Randy's domain; the dancefloor.

The club goer was immediately mesmerised at the lights above the DJ booth and stage, as they picked out the colours of the dazzling bejewelled fingers of the main man as they nimbly pressed buttons, glided over faders and set the needle, before reaching his hand aloft, a vinyl record spinning miraculously on one vertically pointed finger. The mirror ball above it all then splintered these colours into a million shooting stars off every surface and gyrating body, as they danced to the grooves laid down by Randy Feelgood.

The atmosphere inside the club was euphoric and fizzing with electricity, with Randy pulling the strings. As instructed I mingled with the hand-picked guests. Four hundred of the world's most famous faces were in attendance; stars of stage, screen, music, fashion and art. There were sport stars, models, comedians, entrepreneurs and the beautiful set.

My invite came as something of a surprise. I knew the man of course. Who didn't? I was a young struggling cub reporter for the New York Times and Randy had mentored me through college. I was the only journalist allowed in and I had been coached on the do's and don'ts. 'Wear something nice, dance, take notes, be discreet, have a cocktail and don't reveal anything' I was told. It was a wild night and at some point, I removed some clothing but I kept my word.

Randy Feelgood, an almost mythical being, is now, finally ready to share some of the techniques, styles and secrets that have made him one of the foremost names in the International world of the 'star DJ'. Along the way, Randy the jetsetter, go-getter, playboy and DJ, will introduce you to his VIP room of memories from those hedonistic times.

Contained in these pages are in-depth instructions on how to DJ, from Beginners to Advanced level. How to mix, what songs to play. To gain confidence, to entertain. The styles, the fashion and grooming techniques learnt at the beginning of the Disco era. More than anybody else, Randy Feelgood took the dance scene by the scruff of the polyester, wing collared neck and merged Soul, Funk and Pop into what we now know as Disco.

It was his innovations in culture, music and fashion that was to truly create a phenomenon that still thrives to this day in Clubs, Bars and Dance venues all over the world. Dance music has a lot to thank Randy for, as it constantly evolved into the mainstream, a far cry from its humble beginnings in tiny underground rooms, and old fashioned dance halls during the late Sixties.

If you are of a nervous disposition, then you may need to sit in a comfortable chair, make a cup of tea, not too hot, and seek medical attention. For everybody else, hold on tight for the musical ride of your life!

Express Yourself

'They're doin' it on the moon, yeah. In the jungle too. Everybody on the floor, now. Jumpin' like a kangaroo.'

Charles Wright

'The music industry isn't converging toward dance music. Dance music is dance music. It's been around since disco – and way before disco. But there's different versions of dance music.'

Will.i.am

'To me, the seventies were very inspirational and very influential...With my whole persona as Snoop Dogg, as a person, as a rapper. I just love the Seventies style, the way all the players dressed nice, you know, kept their hair looking good, drove sharp cars and they talked real slick.'

Snoop Dogg

'Someone once said "If you can remember the '80's, you weren't really there." Or was it the '70's? I can't recall. Anyway, I was there and I can remember.'

Randy Feelgood

Radio Randy, early 'Sixties

GREEN ONIONS – BOOKER T AND THE MG'S

SOUL BOSSA NOVA – QUINCY JONES

MOJO QUEEN – IKE &TINA TURNER

REALLY SAYING SOMETHING – VELVELETTES

LAST NIGHT – THE MAR-KEYS

HARD TO HANDLE – OTIS REDDING

I GOT YOU (I FEEL GOOD) – JAMES BROWN

HIT THE ROAD JACK – RAY CHARLES MONEY – BARRETT STRONG

REET PETITE – JACKIE WILSON

Let's begin with a little taster of what I'm talkin' about, with my chronological time line of the music I was groovin' too through the 'Sixties and 'Seventies.

Now these are the songs that I would hear on the radio, and coming out of my sister's bedroom when I was just a little bitty chile of three, four and five.

My sisters Loretta, Rosetta and Henrietta borrowed records from friends, or saved up to buy one at Jack Hobbs' record store over in Brooklyn Heights. Being the youngest, I'd get to hear all these great records; these being, in my opinion, the best ten for shakin' what your mama gave ya. And boy did we four kids shake! Even Mama would join in occasionally as she performed the household chores, and she had a lot to shake. In fact, she'd still be shaking long after the record had finished. Meaty beaty big and bouncy, as my old pals *Slade* would describe her.

A handful of driving Instrumentals in this here list, with some early Motown sounds thrusting in between, seeking attention. These are my own personal Top 10 songs of the time to get your dance floor rockin' in a Soul action, maximum satisfaction situation. If you care to dispute you can check out and drop in to my very own Facebook page and share the joy.

Notice also, I've included a couple of crossover tracks from the late 'fifties. The last two tracks are crossing the bridge from Rock 'n Roll to Soul over the fast-flowing river of blood, sweat 'n tears. Not the band, you understand; they were more of a late 'Sixties experimental group, playing Jazz, Blues and twinkly dinkly fiddly stuff. And occasionally investigating the contents of their belly buttons. No, I'm talking about 'Fame Academy' stylin' blood sweat 'n tears.

There's a couple of Soul/Jazz cuts on my list too, with a slice of citrus on the glass to add a little Latin twist, which always bubbled under the Soul movement.

Chapter 1

Can you feel the force?

Whatever music that hooks you, any young blade and dancin' chick knows, you gotta *feel* the beat, if you're gonna move your feet!

It's the mantra I've lived my life by ever since I heard the radio for the first time sat in my mother's kitchen, in my high chair, chewing on a piece of hard biscuit and making a gloopy mess of the whole thing!

Ma was already kitchen-busy, hoovering up the crumbs of my sisters' breakfast after they'd gone to school, and the vacuum cleaner's snake-like hose was a-writhing around the kitchen floor, doing its stuff as *'What I'd Say'* by Ray Charles squeezed itself like a sweet perfume from the little box next to the wilting plant on the windowsill. I stopped what I was doing (dribbling globules of mush all over my bib. Well there ain't much else to do when you're strapped in) and let the rhythms soak through my soft infantile bones. Then I began to bang along, sending extra crumbs southwards!

Mama was as mad as a thirsty hound dog eating hot chilli sauce, but this kid was hooked!

I loved that Ray Charles hipster with his *'I Got a Woman'*, and *'Mess Around'* and all his hits, and my favourite Christmas present that year was a long player that my second sister, Rosetta brought home one day and wrapped up for me. We had nothing to play it on though, so I had to wait 'til next spring when she came home with a big ol' red Dansette record player that she'd mysteriously swapped for some of my Daddy's pistols.

As well as that record, the radio became my best compadre and I was like a dry sponge, soaking up all the moisture I could in a musical sense; from Country to Rock, Calypso to Psychedelic and Boogie Woogie to Garage. I dug the Motown sound and Blues, Atlantic Soul and Jazz, too as I grew up from tiddler to toddler to teen.

So, here I am today, sitting on the balcony on the third-floor basement of my mock Colonial Villa overlooking the Pacific Ocean, not quite ready yet to hang up my cravat and headphones, and being pestered by my main man Hunter to share the know-how and expertise that I have gained in a lifetime of crowd pleasing, floor filling and generally taking the human race on a journey through Soul, D.I.S.C.O. and beyond.

On the way, we'll enter the dives and meet the divas, and the characters. We'll get acquainted with the movers, shakers and trend-setters that helped to shape the movement of the moment, as it was, and we'll dig the scene and get hot and sweaty.

I'll take you through a step by step guide to being a DJ. Not as good as me obviously, but how to play a tune, stick another one on. Then glance, and admire the effect you're having on your adoring audience, and also check out the motions and emotions of all the groovers out there. Some fine-looking players out there, huh?

And all through, I'm gonna give you my Top 10 dancing records of each particular year, as a kinda reference guide for your own particular gig. You got to know your music and I'm teachin' so listen up.

Time to get funky, y'all. Time to *play that funky music white boy.* Or black chick, yellow girl, red squaw...it makes no difference.

That's it, go on. Stick a record on! Are you moving? Is anyone diggin' it? Turn it up! Open the window. Are people dancing? If they are, then you are DJing!

But wait. No, there's a whole heap more to it than just standing there, and dropping the needle on a piece of plastic.

You gotta have music throbbing through your veins, arteries, internal and external organs, and your feet.

You need style, brother. You have to look bad, sister. And I mean bad as in good, not bad as in bad.

And you have to recognise that you are in control of the inner ecstasy of every single person in whatever venue, honky tonk, joint, dive, or discotheque that you find yourself in, playing the tunes and doing your thang.

This includes the bus boy, the dancers and the hat check girl. Hell yeah, they deserve a good time, too. Or else they'll be a-moping around the joint, flat-footed with droopy shoulders and a face like a wolf that's gotten too close to a camp fire in the wilderness, and then had the flames beaten out of her by the farmer's daughter. With a big ol' fireman's shovel around the head.

Remarkably, this describes a chick I once knew when I was shooting 'Saturday Night Fever' with John Travolta in '77. I was doing a spot of Soul City Walkin', a kind of dancing strut, between takes. I was aware of JT checking out my moves. And who could blame him, he's only flesh and blood. That's when I noticed this shapeless, sexless vagabond hangin' around with a clipboard.

This mousey chick was like a Production Runner, or some kind of inappropriately named profession. Certainly didn't do no running. More of a loose-limbed waddle.

But after I got my hands on her she turned from ugly duckling to passable swan. It's all in the posture. You know how to hold yourself in public, and it acts like a chain reaction. I'm talkin' posture, not random self-fondling. If you hold yourself in an upright posture, pushing through gravity and life weariness, you'll look confident, and feel confident. And that'll make you hold your head up and *be* confident.

That girl was like a different person the following week when she walked by my trailer. She'd got her hair done and slapped a bit of make up on, subtle-like, with bright red lips. Don't be shy in using a little assistance in your general appearance, sugar lips. Or else what is the point of livin', huh?

No point. May as well pack up and join a hippie commune and live with the squirrels.

When you is up there in your DJ space you are in control of, and responsible for everyone in the joint's destiny and, of course the destiny of all the groovers, funkateers and in-crowd for the next few joyous hours of their pitifully short existence on this spinning orb in space. So you may as well look your finest.

You have your finger on their collect drive button and it is time to press 'Go'.

You will learn through these here pages, via the biological mysteries of osmosis and reading, how to play the music. You'll learn how to ooze confidence and deliver the best damn tunes in your own unique style, or mine, but that's cool baby, whilst also looking fine and feelin' divine.

When I say feelin' divine, I ain't talking about the he-be/ she-be Drag Queen and singer, Divine. Walk like a man? Good luck with that one, my friend. But more of him and her later.

Radio Randy, mid 'Sixties

BEGGIN' – FRANKIE VALLI

GOING TO A GO GO – THE MIRACLES

TAINTED LOVE – GLORIA JONES

NOWHERE TO RUN – MARTHA AND THE VANDELLAS

WADE IN THE WATER – MARLENA SHAW

CHILLS & FEVER – TOM JONES

SATISFACTION – OTIS REDDING

HARLEM SHUFFLE – BOB & EARL

ROADRUNNER – JUNIOR WALKER

AIN'T TOO PROUD TO BEG – THE TEMPTATIONS

Check out the powerful Soul cuts in this tiny menu. Pounding beats and throat-ripping vocals with a little Gospel vibe. Yowser, yowser, yowser! And you might know some of these slices from remakes and samples. There's even a couple o' covers in there, too for your main course and *'Roadrunner'* for dessert.

The whole lot bookended with records just beggin' to be heard. The original version of *'Tainted Love'* I've included here. A Northern Soul, speed ball, foot-stomper with a fast tempo and baggy pants. Otis works his magic on a Rolling Stones classic. And you may recognise the opening of *'Harlem Shuffle'* which was sampled by House of Pain on *'Jump Around'*.

Chapter 2

I Love Music, any kind of music

Before we get started, it's kinda crucial you dig the music scene. So here's a little beginner's history lesson about its evolution from early Soul, which in itself had its roots in Negro spiritual slave songs, Folk and Gospel. It then had a little whirlwind romance with Doo Wop, via a flirtation with Jazz which sorta steamrollered parallel to the Rock scene.

At about the same time early Blues evolved into Boogie Woogie, and also crashed into Jazz. Bear with me musicologists, 'cos this is where it gets in'eresting, but complicated. And we'll skip past the Barbershop scene (but we may return to those pole fellas at a later date). Throw in a little Calypso, Salsa and Pop. Mix it all up in a Soul food stew with Rhythm and Blues, Motown and Atlantic Soul and it all shoots off in a fountain of genres; Northern Soul, Funk, Pop and finally Disco.

Of course, from there it's off again back once more to a more soulful sound or getting its jiggy on for Street sounds and Rap and House and Hip-Hop and Rare grooves and on and on to New Jack Swing, etcetera.

But what is Disco? I hear you ask. You could say that Disco is defined by soaring vocals, with a steady four on the floor beat. Many songs will have the hi–hat, which is a cymbal on a stand, tapping on a static cymbal meeting it on its downward journey. This will be a rat-a-tatting along with a syncopated bass thrum. But that's too generalised and simplified. You'll also get a lush string sound, or horns, or synthesisers. I have drummer friends, who like to have this cymbal stand slung low, to get more face time. Then you got yourself a lo-hat.

Sometimes you don't need no instruments at all. In fact, Donna Summer's *'I Feel Love'* is the first record entirely devoid of instruments. A pure computer generated dance record that inspired many Electronic bands in the late 'Seventies, including New Order. Check out *'Blue Monday'*. That cut sits hand in sweaty, infectious hand - but not in a diseased way - with *'I Feel Love'*.

Like I said, that track is made entirely by machines, 'cept if you listen very carefully to the production you might hear some jazz triangle in the mix there, courtesy of you know who.

But it all starts with Soul. It's in all of it. And it's in all of me. And it was in the first Prehistoric cave man who pulled out the guts of some roaring sabre-tooth tiger, and then left 'em all dangling on a tree by the cave entrance to cure.

Well, Mrs. Cave man didn't want no chitlins slippin' and slidin' all over her newly swept floor, now, did she?

Anyways, up steps ol' Neanderthal Ned. He's got a heap o' jobs he's been told he should be getting along with, but he can't find his list. He distinctly remembered getting a burnt stick of charcoal and scratchin' out a few words on a passing lizard. But the lizard has slithered off to fight the buzzards for some gizzards and anyway Ned can't read.

Feelin' restless, he goes out and strums on some dangly bits of guts, and it twangs all right, having been dried in the sun.

'Hmm, sounds interestin', he thinks to himself. 'Hey, man', he hollers over to his pal, Stoner Stan. 'Check this out, Stan, my man. I'm strumming this piece o' offal here, and then I twangs this bit next to it and it's at a higher pitch, or like a different note altogether.'

'Ug', comes the reply.

'Seriously, "Ug"? Quit jivin' me man, going all, "Ug", that is so last millennium, dude.'

'Ug...ug...Hey sorry, man. I was just trying to drop these here slippery innards down in one swallow, and I kinda gagged. Hey but, cool sound, man. It's sorta like a twing, and a twang. Let me add a little rhythm here.'

And he grabs a couple of sticks, and its boom, chig-a-boom, chig-a-boom, chig-a-boom, on a moss-covered rock with a couple of sticks. Then another guy wanders into the clearing having heard this crazy beat.

'Er, that music is totally fly my mo-fo's. Hey, you wanna start a band? I got mah own horn.' And he pulls a conch shell outta his loincloth; which must've been painful, somewhat, and he starts blowin' up a screeching pattern.

He's no Miles Davis, but the bass notes are hitting the spot, right in the ribs as they play counterpoint through the twanging and the banging. And that, my friends is the origins of Jazz. Right on, brothers.

Of course, as usual, this attracts a couple of other guys pulled by aural gravity and the crazy rhythm. New guy pesters the newly formed beat combo, and offers some advice.

'Hey, hey, I'm like totally digging your vibe, my bronze-age brothers, but, er, maybe you wanna try hitting that rock with this here chiselled down animal shin bone. It'll give you a fuller sound for your skins.

'Hey, no way, early man. I'm a sticks guy,' says the drummer, and he starts beating on the rock and scatting.

'A-bee bop a boogie, and a dippy dippy doodie, skittly-up, skittly dit, skitty dee dah dah dah dah....'

Mrs. Caveman enters the scene now, sweeping out the cave and earwigging what's goin' on.

'You fellas stop foolin' around with my supper. And Ned, you get your hairy carcass in here, 'n chop some o' these prehistoric vegetables 'fore they just about become extinct.'

Brief History lesson over, but you can get a flavour of my jive from my year on year, best of, top 10 tunes that'll keep the floor jumpin' and your humps a-humpin'.

But relax. I'm only starting at 1960. But a little-known fact is that Rhythm and Blues began hundreds of years earlier. And I'll get to that somewhere down the line if cocktails and dancing ladies don't carry me off on the *Highway to Hell*, or the *Stairway to Heaven*.

Radio Randy 1966/67

IN THE BASEMENT – ETTA JAMES

GET READY – THE TEMPTATIONS

YOU KEEP ME HANGIN' ON – THE SUPREMES

THESE BOOTS ARE MADE FOR WALKING – NANCY SINATRA

HOLD ON I'M COMING – SAM AND DAVE

LAND OF A THOUSAND DANCES – WILSON PICKETT

THE BEAT GOES ON – BUDDY RICH

PAPA'S GOT A BRAND NEW BAG – JAMES BROWN

COME SEE ABOUT ME – JUNIOR WALKER

SAVE ME – ARETHA FRANKLIN

Oh, man alive! Now we're cooking on gas, honey! We is talking 'Year Zero' stuff here. Right about now is when Soul exploded. Motown dominated. But I tell you, Atlantic records weren't far behind, no sir.

Again, big voices, toe curlers and screamers, not Freddie and the Dreamers. I like it, I like it. You better betcha.

Big old fat slabs of the juiciest cuts all marinated in saucy horns with big mamma vocals.

Chapter 3

Last Night A DJ Saved My Life

Most DJs get hung up on the technicals of DJ-ing. All that boring jive-talking about balancing your needle arm, the weight of the needle, grams, gramophones, slip mats and skid marks…. yawn… anyone still awake? I know I ain't.

Hey, quit it Grandpa, and leave that to the geeks and the nerds, man. Of which more, later, in my section on Nicaraguan nymphomaniacs and horny gimps.

You're up in the booth and you're here to learn so switch your eyes and ears on. Turn on, tune in but don't drop out.

So, first off, lay your platter on the turntable and set the 'PITCH' fader on the zero. You can move this up and down, depending on what speed you want your tune kicking out at. I favour just giving each tune a little extra push by 5 percent.

It's like in the restaurants, you know. You speed up the music on a crowded night and people automatically eat faster. Then you can get another bunch of lucky punters in for another cover, unless you're eating at some fancy-Dan, uptown joint like the Drake Hotel on Park Avenue and 56[th,] where they're playing some violins and strings and suchlike. Then I always holler out to the Maitre D'.

'Turn it up, Garcon, and make it a little heavier on the basslines.' To which he usually responds with a little coquettish giggle and a mock French vibrato.

'But Monsieur Randy Feel-bon sir, mon ami, a-hee-hee. You knows that we have les string quartet, *Beau Jolais*, dans la restaurant ce soir.' And so it goes, that we play out this little ritual once a month.

On this particular night in 1978, the spiritual forces that were inside of me all collided on one magical night.

I smoothed down my shirt, and gently dabbed at the corners of my mouth with a linen napkin (It's got to be linen if you want your food joint to have class and credibility).

Then I put down my lobster. I don't know why I brought him with me that night, the Drake has a "strictly no pets" policy.

So, I put Larry back in his basket, fed him some French fries to settle him and excused myself from my dinner companions, Delores Pugh and Brandy Matthews. They were a couple of film actresses that I was escorting round town just then. I was offering a two for one offer I remember, and I'd also brought along a juicy young dancer I had working a couple of slots at The Paradise Club, named Madelaine. I liked her style, using just the one name. Like Cher or Bianca or Superman. Hot and firm and thigh muscles that could crack heads. In fact, she dislocated my right ear once as we swung in my hammock. She went on, as we know to be one of the hottest singers on the planet throughout the '80s thru to the noughties.

I raised a hand to indicate a five-minute dinner interlude, rinsed my mouth out with a crème de menthe cocktail, gargling loudly to get my voice box lubricated and spat it out into the tartare sauce pot. Which can only have improved the flavour, in my opinion. Then I sauntered, apologetically up to the little stage.

I stood the cellist aside, with a gentle hand pressing firmly in the small of her back, saucily slipping a finger down to tweak at her panties and escorted her over to the piano, off to one side next to some palms. Once there, she starts to finger away, (which you couldn't blame her for, being in my presence) at the keys, and gets a little Boogie Woogie rhythm going, while I stand with one lizard-skin Cuban heel on the body of the cello and slap out a fast, bluesy pattern on the top strings.

As I recall, it was kinda like a mixture of *'Midnight Rambler'* by the *Rolling Stones*, with the slappin' fat bass beat from the Headhunters' *'God made me Funky'*, but sped up.

The three chicks with the fiddles picked up on this and shook loose a hypnotic bluegrass melody. Then we settled into a Funk groove, much to the delight of the crowd that was in that night, who were squeezed in to the fancy restaurant at the hotel. I was layin' down some fat 'n funky vibes on the cello that evening, with my hand cavorting and slapping and caressing over the neck and body of that giant instrument, reminding me of a night I spent in the VIP room of the Cobra rooms with some dancers, high on champagne and acid and the *Three Degrees*, one time.

I remember the rock band *Queen*'s road crew were in that night, watching and enjoying the entertainment (at the Drake, that is, not the Cobra rooms).

They was all dressed up in top hat, tails and sneakers with their limos parked out front (the roadies, not the *Three Degrees*). Those guys earned more than *Queen* in those days and employed their *own* road crew to lug the band's gear to and from concerts! Crazy, man.

Where was I? Was I fingering away behind the palms with the cellist? No, that was another night.

Oh Yeah, I remember, so anyway I'm laying down some fine bass jams in a funky punky reggae party Jazz affair before we settled in to a groove with the diners all going wild and the cutlery clattering in time with the beat.

Well, my great friend, the *Funkadelic* high priest, George Clinton was in that night, at the top table with his big old hair flapping around, and I just knew I'd turned him onto the groove. He was beaming all over his whiskery chops as he cavorted around the place, whipping up the diners to the max, before grabbing the mic to sing freestyle, making up rhymes and melodies to weave in and out of the strings.

Man, that dude could funk it. We did a call and response thing, whilst the girls harmonised improv style. I could see Lucien, the Maitre D' weeping in the corner by the kitchen door by now, so I pulled the horn and we somehow managed to turn that eighteen-wheeler of a monster sound into the parking lot for a slow climax to give the diners time to adjust their dress and compose themselves for the next course.

I duly obliged by concluding with a little medley of Jazz standards and Barbershop just to restore order.

Then I went over and sat at the Bar to quench my appetite with a Calypso Pina Colada and Ouzo et Dubonnet, some exotic dancers I knew from Studio 54.

Next day Clinton calls me up. George that is, not Hilary. That was just a rumour. Which I cannot corroborate, though she was a fine lookin' chick back in the day. And George was spouting forth about what a great night he'd had.

'Randy, I pick up on styles, way before they get popular, pretty much before young kids do. I see 'em coming.' And you better believe it, that guy started out in doo wop, dabbled in a Motown sound, then developed his Funk muscles with Parliament and Funkadelic before hitting on the Hip Hop scene. He was an innovator, for sure.

That jam eventually turned into *'One Nation under a Groove'* by his *Funkadelic* band.

Little did I know but a few other cats were in that night, too. *Queen's* bass player, John Deacon also got hip to the dip of the bass trip and wrote *'Another one Bites the Dust'* which came out in '80, whilst the band was listening at the back door. They couldn't afford the Drake's cover charge back then, and just skulked around the back, eating take-away Chinese, according to Freddie, while their roadies ordered dessert and brandy. Different times, baby.

My bass man Bernard Edwards swore that the *'Deac-duke'* stole the riff from his band, *Chic*'s *'Good Times'*. But Bernie was at the Drake too that night too, so who's zooming who?

And cock an ear to Paul Simon, but not when he's rambling on about local South African rhythms and diamonds ground into your boots again. Those gems 'll get your toes tapping for sure. With impatience. Talk about a carbon footprint, huh? Get yourself some rubber soles, my friend, and wear the diamonds around your neck, or on a finger.

No, I mean listen up to *'Late in the Evening'* which also came out in 1980. I can hear a little bit of old Randy comin' atcha, sho' nuff, with that pulsating salsa rhythm.

Late in the evening, and indeed during the day, in the '70s was a time when Disco exploded all over the music scene and 'cos I was there at the beginning, all the cats thought I'd invented it.

I did, of course, in a way. But I always replied to that with my usual throwaway comment of 'woulda happened anyway, dude. I just gave it a little nudge and a tweak in the right direction, funk wards, just as I would to an inquisitive child.'

Just as I did with Randy Junior in fact when he showed an interest in golf ball diving.

Everyone was collaborating back then, and I was sought out for my essence and maracas. You can hear my work on most of those records that came out of New York in the late '70s. Mostly Disco, but I also did some studio time with some Rock acts, too; *Stones*, *Zeppelin*, *Rod Stewart* and the *Stray Cats* amongst them.

I also provided some backing vocals on *'Love to Love You Baby'*, but that was by accident.

I was having me some afternoon delight, with an actress friend of mine, Cleopatra James. She was one statuesque sister. Same height as me at six-one and broad in the shoulder. Could ha' been an Olympic swimmer with those fine broad shoulders, or a weightlifter, and this gave her cleavage a certain lift and separation. What a gal.

We'd been flirting on and off for a while, with little lingering looks and naked wrestling at Bazookas. Time is tight and the moment was right, and we managed to squeeze in a matinee at my pad one day. Whilst we was getting' it on under the glass coffee table I must have accidently kicked my trim phone and dialled up Georgio Moroder who was working with Donna Summer just then.

I had called him up that very morning to help him in his ambition to create a more European variation of Disco. I suggested moustaches. Anyway, I must have knocked the redial button with my foot during my passion. Georgio was out, thank God, probably surfing on the west coast, and the sounds of our heavy-petting somehow made it on to his answer machine and the final pressing. Edited down of course. The album version was only seventeen minutes long and it took me fifteen just to work up one of Cleo's hot, ripe nubbins.

She was a big girl, my Cleo. Amazonian, and her fine dark skin was glistening that night on my thick Persian rug. Still had her thigh-high boots on and little else as we rolled around pressing the flesh. A tall lady as I said, and everything was in perfect proportion, only bigger. Two enormous firm breasts stood proud from her torso, a fine slim waist with just a little softness in the belly and downy soft hair below. And strong, long legs seemingly carved from mahogany. Firm from lots of dancing. She also sported tight independently moving butt cheeks. The type you just can't stop grabbing hold of and massaging firmly and fondly. Especially when she's driving you home with her heeled boots in your behind.

She was a goddess, and I prayed at her altar that afternoon, remembering to take my shoes off first before bowing my head and sipping from the cup as it was offered.

Well, we made it on to Donna's record, alright, and I've continued to have that magical ability to influence and improve on projects which I've been involved with.

I've also done some consultation gigs on some of the big Musical movies during that time; *'Saturday Night Fever', 'Thank God it's Friday', 'Blues Brothers', 'Caligula'* and more.

There's a heap of session time just itchin' to be told, but we'll leave the Rock and the Movies and 'Eighties for another time; we're doing Soul, Funk, Disco here. The three sisters of Dance.

[Author's note – Cleopatra James left New York in 1976 and became a personal body guard to King Busawela of the Fasonagbo province in Africa and was famed for her statuesque beauty and military cunning. She had a unique way of dispatching King Busawela's enemies; with her thighs.]

Radio Randy 1967/68

SOUL MAN – SAM AND DAVE

TRAMP – OTIS REDDING & CARLA THOMAS

RESPECT – ARETHA FRANKLIN

SWEET SOUL MUSIC – ARTHUR CONLEY

MUSTANG SALLY – WILSON PICKETT

I LIKE IT LIKE THAT – PETE RODRIGUEZ

BIG BIRD – EDDIE FLOYD

LOVE MAN – OTIS REDDING

CHAMP – THE MOHAWKS

DANCE TO THE MUSIC – SLY AND THE FAMILY STONE

Starting to get a smattering of poppy/Latino styles in the mix now. But still a heavy Soul sound and these Artistes will hammer you into submission. If you ain't pounding the floor and movin' your hips then you is deader than a dodo's doings, brothers and sisters.

Eddie Floyd has a slight interaction here with the San Francisco west coast Hippy scene. And with my friend Sly, you get a bit of everything; Funk, Rock, Soul, Disco, Psychedelia, nice 'n sleazier. He'd bung in a bit of Ragtime too, if he could get away with it.

Chapter 4

Don't Stop Til You Get Enough

So, back to the tutorial. Come on, concentrate and stop getting me all reminiscing. Now stick your headphones on and listen to the tune before you go 'live', with the output fader down, 'CUE' button on.

Cue it up by physically pushing your vinyl around 'til the needle picks up the sound. Set your 'Fader' up.

Whack it in, then line up the next tune on the other turntable. When you're starting out, practice with the same record, but in duplicate form, you dig? Just have two records the same, something like *'I Want Your Love'* by *Chic*. With this song, you have a definite 1,2,3,4 drumbeat to guide you in, nice 'n easy does it.

When you've gained a little confidence, start thinking about mixing a different tune in. More of that later, too.

Feel the groove, feel the beat and know your music. No, I mean *really know your music!*

What is the tune that'll fit with this track? Is it the same beat, or BPM? (Beats per minute). Is it in the same key? Will it be a seamless mix rhythmically? Does it have maracas? OK, how about a drumbeat? Tambourine? Bongos? Man, don't ever neglect the bongos.

Cool. Be sure to check my mixing ideas for your playlists, at the end section of my book.

Mix it in on the other turntable by practising scratching it in. Try and match up the bass beat, or a drum beat, something definable.

When you've done all of that, like, a hundred times, unplug your turntables, roll up all that spaghetti mess of cables and things. Then carefully lay it all out in a small, cushioned dumpster and wheel them round to the Smithsonian museum, man!

Get yourself a CD Mixing Desk. That's the future, right there.

This'll blow your mind. Your mixing will be seamless, the Cue is instant and the song will come in at the correct speed, and without all that nasty crackling and spitting that sounds like someone's cooking eggs and bacon when the oil's too hot!

Ouch! Think it just spat hot fat in my eye! Which reminds me of the time I was hosting a private party with Barry White and the New York Giants Cheerleaders I had staying at my apartment just then.

I'd been coaching them girls for a few weeks and they just about begged me to put 'em in my second bedroom with the full-length mirror on one wall (and ceiling) to practice.

So, we're at my Private Club 'Bazookas' next door to The Paradise on 53rd. Barry had some of his 'Love Unlimited' band in that night, and let me tell you, they is inappropriately named. After just a couple of hours of jammin' and partyin' they all started to run out of love-steam and one by one snuggled down on my pashmina rugs and beanbags and curled up spooning their brass. So, by two in the morning, we had to carry on the party with just me and the Cheerleaders and a cup of iced snow.

Man, we went through some moves that night, with that big ol' hunk-a-hunk, a-burnin' lover blubber man, Barry passed out on the couch snoring his big bassy nostrils all over the place. Added to that soundtrack, Puffing Willy, the sax man, slept with his lips round his own horn (a neat trick if you can do it). He was blowing in rhythm with the walrus of love. Still sounded romantic, though, and was the rhythm to some athletic lovin', with pom-poms.

So anyways, you gotta be careful mixing some of them vinyl 45's in, and you better believe it, sugar, some of them cuts from the 'Seventies, the beat is all over the place, too. It's like they was producing high, but with their socks on the down stroke.

Take *'Carwash'* for instance by them British dudes, Rose Royce. You got the handclapping on a beat, then the Bass player, turns up. He's late for the session and just starts slapping away at his axe, all speeded up, but creating a nice groove and leaving the clappers to play catch up.

Well, you try mixing to that crazy mis-timed engine and you gotta have your wits about ya and a steady finger on that pitch fader.

Of course, back in the day we knew no different, so vinyl was the thing and you had to dig it, man, or you was corduroy. But as I look back now, over the summer haze that's floating over the Californian Paradise Hills and the valley below, from my cream and burgundy balcony, I can appreciate how hard it was to be a DJ back then.

Not for me, naturally. I was like a pinball wizard, without the deaf, dumb and blind bit....and with more class. I was the baton-wielding conductor of my own orchestra; mixing and matchin', and despatchin' the scratchin'.

But back then I was a pioneer of the idea, and a couple of Chinese superfreak, master geeks set me up with a custom-built CD 'rack and stack' mixing desk with a champagne bottle/maracas combination holder and shelf attachment. Mind-blowing, daddio.

I got to know these techno kids whilst I was going through my Kung Fu fighting period, when we was working out at the same gym, El Tony's in Brooklyn back in '74. El Tony was a big Tex-Mex dude from south of the border. Running all kinds of scams outta his gym, particularly gambling. And the Chinese will bet on just about anything. Two flies buzzing round the room? They'll bet on that action. So, these dudes came along with their gadgets one night as I was adjusting my belt.

Man, them black haired, slick kickers really knew their stuff, and I road-tested that star-ship console for them at my invitation gigs around the States in the early '80s. They'd managed to transfer all my vinyl onto CDs with some mysterious Oriental wizardry. But I still kept my old records just in case something didn't click.

So, you're in front of your Desk. 'oh man, not this crap again', I hear ya holler, head in your hands. Just go with it, dude. We're nearly done with the whole teaching tutorial thang. I'm itching to get at my half-drunk Mojito over on my private bar, here. And that is one sultry Jezebel I can't leave 'til she gets fully satisfied, you dig?

So just hang on in there, and stick your CD in your Denon player or whatever. Hit 'PLAY', with the fader down, so only you can hear it through your headphones. Now stick another CD in the other player. Same thing; feel the beat, move your feet and your best friend is the 'PITCH' fader. Anything'll mix if you use it right!

Set your 'GAINS', that's the individual volume control at the top. Set 'em up to '11', maximum; get it up there. Then adjust your bass, mid and treble at '12 o'clock' to begin. As you become accustomed, you can play around with your knob, oh yeah, but be discreet.

You can also adjust your control buttons as you play different tunes with questionable recording quality. Some, you'll need to get the mid and top right on full to get the most outta the track, example being *Rescue Me'*, Fontella Bass. But be minded to set it back for the next one or you'll have a front row of bleeding eardrums, and Club owners are not keen on that scenario, sucker!

Set your 'MASTER' volume to midway at first and make sure that bitch boy, bar hop has turned all the amps on and up in that little secret amp cupboard/ love shack where it's dusty and hot and with a little buzz going on. Mighty dangerous to stick around too long in that room. I always kept a few scatter cushions inside and kept my visits down to a manageable two minutes, start to finish, and everyone was happy!

Especially Lindy Bell, a regular at The Coconut. She'd strut right in with her high heels on and long tight dress, looking all seductive with her girlfriends. Then she'd have some martinis and I could see she was ready.

'Lindy, it's time, honey', I'd call out over the microphone, during a break in the lyric, naturally.

That was Lindy's cue to strip off the cumbersome, sheer gown, right down to her sexy black lingerie, while still in her heels. Those lacey things looked so fine against her tight alabaster little body. Then she'd prowl around the entire circumference of the club with a sassy look on her foxy face with her wavy hair wafting behind.

That was her thing. She was an exhibitionist. And the Coconut practically encouraged that. Well I did, anyways.

Radio Randy 1969

IT'S YOUR THING – THE ISLEY BROTHERS

PURPLE HAZE – JOHNNY JONES & THE KING CASUALS

FOR ONCE IN MY LIFE – STEVIE WONDER

THE SNAKE – AL WILSON

THINK – ARETHA FRANKLIN

I GOT YOU BABE – ETTA JAMES

TWENTYFIVE MILES – EDWIN STARR

SQUEEZE ME – DYNAMIC 7

SPOOKY – DUSTY SPRINGFIELD

SOUL LIMBO – BOOKER T AND THE MG'S

'There's a giant sale on this weekend at McGregor's nightwear and lingerie Emporium; Lexington and twenty-third. You don't need Pajamas at Rosie's, but you can buy yours cheap this weekend. Fifty percent off on many lines. Sale starts Saturday, you snooze, you lose!'

This is where things start getting mighty interesting music-wise. You got the soulful sound of Dusty with her silky smooth vocal, the usual suspects ripping out your eye balls with their throats and the foot-stomping Northern Soul sound breaking through. Open the door, get on the floor, everybody walk the dinosaur. But make sure you got your pajamas on!

Chapter 5

Fingertips (Parts 1&2)

CD's made life somewhat easier for the DJ back then. There was less to carry around for one thing. Instead of boxes and crates covered with nice satin, or velour fabrics, I needed only my big old CD wallet with little slots for all my discs.

But what I loved most about playing vinyl, was the visual aspect. I could entertain with a move, a groove or a visual interlude. I could stick a finger in the air and dazzle the masses with my disc-spinning trick.

This was just showmanship on my part, wanting to create another treat for the boppers and bangers out there. It was simply a false finger from my friend, Wizard Woody's *'magic shop and plumbing store'* over in Manhattan.

So, you stick a little axle off a 'matchbox' car through the tip of a false finger and attach this wheel to a vinyl long player by melting it to the plastic. I had to practice this bit a couple of times with some of my sister's rare Sam Cooke long-players 'til I got it right with no kinks or warps.

Then you set your middle finger in the falsey, set the record spinning and hold your hand aloft, finger pointing skywards, as if to pronounce 'right on.' It was a mixture of devilment and jiggery-pokery that I learned from my friend, Keith Moon.

I was practising off and on. The spinning, not the melting the plastic all over Loretta's kitchen sides thing, and I just couldn't get it right. I had the prop, as they say in the movie business. But I couldn't get my fingers working as I wanted. It was a work in progress 'til I bumped into the master drumstick twiddler himself.

I'd met Keith, or *Brave Sir Robin* as I called him (I was a big fan of the Monty Python guys and just loved Keith's English accent) at an after show party that I'd been asked to DJ at, in some Club near Central Park, called The Palace.

It was owned by Penelope Field, a chick from England who'd graduated from Cheltenham Ladies College, then married a Saudi Prince. She saw off the horny old-timer with her inventive gymnastics in the boudoir in one of his Palaces in the desert. They breed some healthy young ladies at those all girl's private schools, yes sir. The kind who are all sass and wanton lower lip.

She came back to the Big Apple with a stack of cash and bought The Palace. It was all decked out with expensive rugs and Arabian designed couches and large bean bags all scattered around. And there were erotic paintings of Middle Eastern veiled ladies hung on every wall. Great glass bowls of fruit, coke, chocolate fondue and even small wrapped candy chews lined the tables along one wall; fruit salads and black jacks, four for a penny. Which was Penelope's little joke as it was common knowledge that Penelope had insatiable and exotic tastes when it came to the bedroom, or the garden. She was no stranger to pulling a train. And men were literally queueing up for her delights. Everyone called her *'Four for a Penny'* and that's how much those little wrapped sweets cost in the store.

All the in crowd were there for the after show, that night. There were Rock stars, and Soul singers, movie stars and models, hookers and moneymen and I was enjoying hobnobbing whilst still working the wheels of steel and sharing a pipe with James Hunt, the British racing driver.

I spotted Keith, who was on great form that evening, playing the fool and taking a large swallow from everyone's drinks if they'd just put 'em down on a table. He was always on the lookout for some kind of mischief.

Out of my peripheral vision I saw him reach out for my tumbler just as I was coming out of *'Running Away'* by Roy Ayres, easing in *'Movin'* by *Brass Construction* and lining up the next groove, *T-Connection*'s *'Do What You Wanna Do'*.

Now I'll briefly pause my little tale to talk records here, if you'll allow me. And why wouldn't cha, It's my story.

So, it was a fairly showbizzy affair and it wasn't particularly necessary to have the dance floor bumper to bumper. It was a free bar and spirits were high.

I was tootling along in my own unique groove playing some Jazz-Funk, and they don't get any better than my man, Roy Ayres. *'Running Away'* is a chillin', Soul-tinged Jazz number with an insistent vibraphone hook just oozin' pheromones. Just like your humble guide. Except I ain't actually humble.

He virtually invented the concept of Jazz-Funk. His speciality was the vibraphone instrument. It's a kind of a xylophone keyboard thing with a smooth sound that he'd just lay his little rubber tipped stick things on. Then weave the sound in and out of his compositions like a Bayeux Tapestry monk high on mead and nuns and Medieval chanting, creating a blissful groove.

I taught him a couple of tricks for a heavier sound, like attaching a wire brush onto the frets of your Bass, and tipping your hat at a more frivolous angle. This was during some studio down-time when I was laying down some tracks for Bowie. I think he dug me, but the man's a maestro and can do no wrong in my mind.

So, there I was, playin' *'Running Away'*, *doo be doo, run, run, run*, then I gently mixed and slapped in *Brass Construction*, a timeless piece of insistent Funk instrumental but with Soul backing singer accompaniment. Then came my big banger of that particular vibe, *'Do What You Wanna Do'*.

What a fine funky mash; but again, starts off slow with a bass riff pumping along then it picks up the pace as the band gets into the swing. It's a mighty fine example of 'Funk Prog' as I like to call it. The band getting down to the jam and playing off each other, and it fit perfectly with the mood of the evening.

I was concentrating with one hand on the record and my other trying to ride the pitch fader whilst holding off Penelope next to me at arm's length with my stockinged toe. She was trying to wrap herself around my leg at the time with her silk gown accidently, but on purpose, slipping over her shoulders. She had her glittery love pillows squashed up against my knee and an erotic look in those bewitching eyes, boring into me under hooded lids.

Keith had his hand on my Tequila Sunrise and Champagne combo at the same time, and I was thinking to myself, 'hot dang, Randy, here we go again. Everyone wants a piece of your ass.'

And I just managed to grab Keith's wrist, which was no easy task, I can testify. He had a unique jazz style of drumming while smashing the devil outta those petrified skins. Thus, his lower arms and hands had an almost bionic power.

I settled *T-Connection* down with my chin on the Pitch Fader, and tried to ignore Penny doing the hot and sweaty Rumba at my feet, with my satin pants unbuttoned and her hands doing their deliciously wicked work, before Keith could knock multi-coloured bubbles all over my silk vest or worse.

His fingers were strong as steel, whereas Penny's were soft and nimble, and he broke my grip instantly by contorting his fingers around mine like they were snakes in a bag, wriggling and going off and snapping away.

It was then that I recognised the dude; the legendary drummer with the *Who*, with his sweat-streaked mop hair and big puppy dog eyes with a mad but happy visage. I liked the guy and after I'd extricated myself from Penelope's fingers, we got to talking and he invited me up to his Hotel room the very next day.

'Come for breakfast' he said, 'about 4 o'clock. Let's call it a high tea-breakfast.' Sounded A-OK to me and I continued doing my thang, after adjusting my wardrobe just in time for the wig-out instrumental bit of *'Do What You Wanna Do'*, where the bongos kick in and the psychedelia-drenched Hammond organ gets all beautifully jazzy. That gave me time to properly finish off Penny to gain some peace.

Then I rapped over it with some rhymes I'd been working on with some friends of mine who performed street dancing and jive rapping in Harlem at the time.

'I said a hippety hop, a hippety hop

Do the hip, then hop you don' stop a rock it

To the bang bang boogie, say, up jump to boogie

To the rhythm of the boogie the beat'.

I'd become acquainted with a sassy sister, name of Sylvia Robinson, back then. She'd had minor successes as a Soul artist and was now whipping these boys into shape for a new kinda sound she was creating.

She wanted me to test drive these rhymes to check out the vibe in a Club setting. And some of it featured on *The Sugarhill Gang*'s smash hit *'Rapper's Delight'* the following year when they fused the lyric with *Chic*'s *'Good Times'*. Man, was Nile spitting feathers when I saw him next day. He was so angry, he'd chewed his pillow half to death. His copyright had been by-passed and *sampling* as we now know it, took off from there.

What a record. Recognised as the first proper Hip Hop/Rap song. But I'm sure my *Incredible Bongo* buddies would dispute that.

As would Ian Dury who rapped on most of his own tracks. *'Hit me with your Rhythm Stick'*, hell yeah.

So, I did this little rap as a favour to the boys, and Sylvia. They knew I was cool and always wore neutral gang colours when venturing north of Central Park. In fact, I nearly created my own gang, the Peacocks, on account of the rainbow of colours I always wore. Sometimes it's all about the badge you is wearing. And you gotta be wise or prepare for a surprise. One time I was getting hit on by a lady-dude cos I had my paisley stunt-cravat just peeping out of my left hand rear pocket of my tight denims. That meant I was a baggage-handler, apparently.

Man, I was on fire, keepin' the crowd a-pumpin' for my next master stroke, *'Love is in the Air'* by John Paul Young. Just to change the mood a little. It was a great night, the kind I love. Surrounded by the beautiful set and limitless supplies of cocktails and fizz.

Next morning, I rose about eleven, and had my usual breakfast shake; my own recipe.

Pineapple, lime, ginger, cranberries, cucumber, apple all spun and cut with my new gadget; a multi-blade Phillips food blender. It makes approximately two tall glasses. I had one myself and put two curly straws in the other for Penelope and her girlfriend for when they arose. It gives you the zing you wanna bring to start your day fresh. And replaces lost fluid, you hear me?

Pineapple is great for the complexion and ginger and lime just gives your blood a little natural shot of energy.

It was a pleasant day so I took a stroll through Central Park, strutting my stuff along the path. It was a Saturday as I recall, and the Park was busy with dudes riding skateboards, and joggers, and girls playing double-dutch, guys hanging out shooting hoops and girls tricked out in summer dresses. The sun was warm and there was a freshness in the air as I tooled along whistling an *Abba* song.

I had my felt Fedora parked at a crazy rakish angle of forty-five degrees, a silk waistcoat with scenes from the Karma Sutra printed on it (a present from Penny), over my *'The Who'* T-shirt (a present from the band) and skin-tight striped flared Guess jeans (a gift from one of Charlie's Angels, who had left them behind in my closet), creating a nice cooling effect on my ankles. I was feeling jazzy and looking snazzy.

As I got to the corner of the block where Keith's Hotel was, I noticed a line of yellow cabs blocking the road. As I approached I could see a heap of smashed wood and stuff all over the asphalt. The cabs were blocking the road along the whole block and I hustled over to one of the bananas on skates [taxi cabs]. I recognised the driver, Bobby D, a young punk who'd done lots of electrical magic with wires and cables and plugs and whatnot at the Coconut Club.

'Hey Bobby D, my main man, what's up and what's going down?'

'Some cat gave us a Benny [a Benjamin Franklin, slang for a $100 note] each, to block the road so he can trash his Hotel room. We all took it. Beats driving around the City collecting rides for a couple of bucks. Crazy mother keeps hoofin' all his furniture out the window up there.' He drew casually on his cigarette, and screwed up his eyes like a grandmother sucking eggs thru an ant's behind. Whilst still drawing, he spat scrags and specks of tobacco out of the side of his mouth. It's a skill, I guess.

'Uh-huh, no jive? What the heck. You gotta love this upside-down town, don't ya? Catch ya later, man.' I said, as nonchalantly as I could and I hustled over to the Doorman, pressed his palm with a dollar (a la 'Top Cat', but without the string attached) and rode the elevator up to find Keith's room. I got there to find the door open and him trying to squeeze the television set over the window ledge.

'Keith, baby. How's it hangin' my man?'

'Ah, Mister Randy, dear boy. You came. How delightful.' He said when he saw me, and the TV kinda slipped through his grasp back on to the floor, with a thud. He invited me over to sit on the sofa, which lay halfway up the wall. We sat on the arm and Keith rang down for room service, while we watched a Western, sideways. The champagne arrived and over the next couple of hours he taught me the drummers trick; how to twirl, twiddle and spin the sticks.

My fingers were burning and aching from all the bending and contorting them around into unnatural positions without any natural lubricant. After a while I asked him if we could practice with an *actual*, physical drumstick.

'I really appreciate the lessons and all, Keith, man, but I need to have context. I'm just fiddling mid-air here. Like I'm pleasuring the *Invisible Woman*, if she was stood on a table changing a lightbulb.' Which is a trick not to be taken lightly, as me and said lady was asked to leave Macey's department store and not upset the furniture display.

Anyway, so back in the Hotel room (with Keith that is, not the *Invisible Woman*) I was plum frustrated at my lack of twirling-time. He looked back at me from the window, and sighed, with a rolled-up shower curtain tucked up under his arm.

'Ah, Randy, baby, it's all visualisation, at the moment. You have to feel the drumstick, be at one with it, like it's an extension of you.'

I was getting a little bent out of shape now, despite his lovely lilting English voice.

'Hey cut the mumbo jumbo crap, man and give me your sticks.' I begged. He calmly chastised me with a raised bushy eyebrow and went all wistful as he slid the shower curtain over the ledge and then gazed out over Central Park, the plastic unfolding like a giant multi-coloured prehistoric, sting ray-like flying devil and flapping downwards to the cordoned off street below.

'I told people I was a drummer before I even had a set. I was a mental drummer.' Then he paused, but seemed to lose the thread. Well I ain't going to argue with the man as he was clearly off his rocker, still.

'And besides,' he said, 'I've just thrown my sticks out of the window. How about using these wooden spoons, dear boy?'

And he whipped two ladles out of the back pocket of his somewhat grimy yellow satin pants.

'Keith Moon is only interested in looking good and being screamed at', said Pete Townsend once. Well, we certainly did a lot of screaming that warm spring afternoon of '78, way up high in an opulent hotel room, as I honed my spinning techniques with those spoons, under Keith's patient tutoring.

I say patient, but in fact we got along mighty fine, with cocktails and Champagne to fuel our endeavours. Oh, and we did have our high tea, too. Little sandwiches, cakes and English tea in fine china cups. And afterwards we threw it all out of the window. Well, it had all been paid for and then some. Saved some poor sucker the washing up, too. I kept the spoons, though, and use 'em to this day.

Every time I whip up some fashionable fruit and vegetable concoction or one of my special cocktails, I think of Keith, that mad crazy fool of a drummin' wizard.

Keith Moon passed away later that year, another friend lost to the demons of showbiz. And I often raise a spoon in silent salute to my loony amigo.

That spinning trick that Keith taught me always got the crowd excited, and my fingering was often requested, particularly by the ladies. I also had a little trick with my cravat, where I learned to take one off with an extravagant flick of the wrist, when it was getting somewhat out of shape and sweat-drenched. Then I'd re-tie another one and, at the same time, undo the brassiere of the showgirl dancing in the podium in front of me.

Titillation and flirtation was all part of the show, baby, for no additional fee. Satisfaction guaranteed – but no refunds!

MOVE ON UP – CURTIS MAYFIELD

HERE COME THE GIRLS – ERNIE K. DOE

SIGNED SEALED DELIVERED – STEVIE WONDER

VEHICLE – THE IDES OF MARCH

OYE COMO VA – SANTANA

SPILL THE WINE – WAR

LITTLE GREEN BAG – GEORGE BAKER

SUPERBAD – JAMES BROWN

ROCK STEADY – ARETHA FRANKLIN

FUNKY NASSAU – BEGINNING OF THE END

The Soul's on hold, temporarily as we explore new avenues and rummage around the bushes, foraging for more funky vibes with some laid back, hippy dippy trippy interludes and bongos. And plucking ripe berries from the fruitful foliage of Funk. But don't get me started on bushes and foliage and ripe berries again, I 've just calmed myself down thinking about Penny's gyrations.

We also got a little Latino groove laid upon ya here with another nod to Northern Soul which became a scene in the north west of England, for a time early '70s. Northern Soul was famous for its all-nighters when kids high on sweat, speed and adrenaline would bop and dance 'til dawn, then strut home to get no sleep. It was all about the urgency of the sound and DJ's had to speed those cuts on to keep the floor.

But for this particular top ten, I is all about mixing it up and seeing what pops out. Keeps music fresh and alive and at any time you gotta be prepared for something popping out, sugar.

Aretha's on fine form with this lolloping funky track and we begin and end the ten with the dual mothers of all horny jams. Or jams with horns in, if you will. And if you will, then I will, too.

'Goobers are delicious peanuts covered in chocolate.'

'Diet Rite Cola, everybody likes it.'

(No, they ain't delicious, and Diet Rite tasted like watery, treacly latrine water, if you ask me.)

Chapter 6

Le Freak!

Get yourself a little gimpy bitch boy.

There's a lot to think about up there in the spotlight, what with giving everybody in the Disco club the time of their life, again and again.

Not least carrying all your paraphernalia up and down stairs, to get into your booth or onto the stage.

You got your microphone, headphones, bucket of ice for the Moet, and the Chandon, (such a great blend when those guys got it together). Then, there's your neck tie tree (I like to do occasional costume changes, depending on the record).

And there's also my record boxes. Some DJs will have a couple of wooden crates, or plastic bucketty type affairs. Well, that is just plain disrespectful to your audience, man! This is an event, and *everything* should be visually appealing, not some junk yard, scrap chat, knick-knack paddy whack, jumble rumble.

Let me lay it on you. Get yourself some thick velvet table cloths. You can get them at any haberdashery store. I import mine from a tiny hamlet in South America. I favoured a deep crimson, or sapphire blue. Classy, right? And I'd display my records at an angle on the bench next to my decks.

When CDs came in it was easier, you know, with them all arrayed in my leopard skin-bound, leather-effect, oversized CD wallet. That thing looked like *'War and Peace'* after Laura Ashley had got her sewing machine all fired up.

I don't need to be doing my own physical humping and bumping when I got a South American, Filipino, or Eastern European dude to do it for me. Just giving something back is all.

I always had a penchant for a young guy, late teens, early twenties, slightly shorter than me, I'm six-one in my silk stockings. So, say between five-ten, five-eleven, yeah and sharp, too. I don't want no guy who's gonna have a slack jaw and a lazy eye. He's got to know where to stick a jacked-cable, or tape up and plug in a loose lead and such like. We're getting down to technicals again, now, and that's an avenue less travelled for an Artiste such as myself.

So, I recruited a couple of Egor's in the early years. Egor One only lasted a couple of months but Egor, Mark II hung around a little longer.

Mighty pasty, being Slavic but I encouraged them to use a little bottle-tanning; a trick I discovered from my mentor Derek Figg, better known as Rico Figaro, and better still, Disco Dick.

But more of him later.

Mario was another dude that I kind of adopted in the role of riding shotgun on the stagecoach DJ booth from Goodtimesville to Outtasighttown, with all stops in between.

Mario was an immigrant from Albania who managed to escape from the oppressive yoke of medieval Communist tyranny in '71. Namely, his battle-axe wife in the Bronx. Yeah there were some crazy times happening in the five boroughs in the early 'Seventies.

He had one scary woman back home, and an even more frightening girlfriend in the next block so was glad to get out from behind the sofa, and high-tail it across the Harlem River. Which he just about managed, disguised as a watermelon.

Yeah, that's right. It was a trick he'd learned when he made his first escape from tyranny. East to west, Albania to Corfu. All the dudes wanting a better life for themselves in Albania would cut a watermelon in half, eat all the juice and stuff inside, then stick the outsidey, husky bit on their head and swim across the mile or so of the Ionian Sea to the Greek Island of Corfu.

Therefore Mario, naturally took the same course of action in coming over to Manhattan, this time with no gun-toting commie gun boat careening down on his ass, just his man-mountain woman. Sad times, brothers, and evidently the bridge must have been out.

He sauntered into the Marabou one afternoon, dripping wet with a watermelon on his head asking for a job. Well, Egor II had just left to lollop back under some cellar, so I was short of a gimp.

'Yeah, alright, dude'. I said. 'But ya gotta lose the headgear.'

'Zank you sorrr.' He beamed back, snot and red mess covering his cheeks.

He was an eager learner, fetching me drinks and carrying my load. He smiled a lot and his olive skin gave him an exotic look. Great hair too, when he wasn't wearing some fruit on his head.

Remember that Ray Stevens song, *'The Streak'*? I'd sing that to old Mario, changing the lyric a little.

'Oh yes, they call him le freak, fastest thing on two feet', etcetera. Nile Rodgers overheard me do that one time, and I swear that's where he got the idea for his *Chic* song. That, and getting chucked outta 54.

But I had to let Mario go in the end. He had a thing for the wrong kind of ladies. You know, the ones with questionable gender in a "is she, isn't she" kind of way. He also favoured ladies who hang around the back of clubs, next to the dumpsters.

'Zay are zo sexy', he'd purr. 'Beggeeeng for eet'.

Dirty dog.

He was a strange dude, right enough. On a day off, he went to a concert, uptown. Later that evening I gets a call from my cop pal, Hank Kowalski to say he had Mario in the cells at Precinct 13.

'What's up Kowalski?' I said, after the waitress had tracked me down to my Jacuzzi over the club. I got her to towel me off before heading down towards the phone.

'We got your boy in the lock up, Randy', he drawled, from underneath his moustache.

'What he done, Kowalski?'

'Got thrown out for stage-diving at Madison Square Garden.' Well, I knew the kid liked his Rock music 'n all, but that was a classy venue and that boy 'll crack his head open, gettin' up to them monkey shines.

'He climbed up on stage, and threw himself out into the auditorium. Very dangerous and violated the venue's strict policy of audience responsibility.' Kowalski continued.

'Which band, Hank'. I said

'Barbara Streisand. Very serious. That kid could have broken his neck, if he hadn't been wearing a hat made of cabbage leaves.' And he rung off after promising me he'd drive him over, minus the hat. Kowalski owed me one, and I guess the free cab ride in a black and white evened us up temporarily.

That Mario dude was just too much. I had to let him go, he was just too high-maintenance and Streisand still ribs me to this day, bringing me an exotic fruit gift each time we meet.

Bobby D. was the best of the rest and we was on the same wavelength, digging the same kind of music. Though he favoured more of a Pop sound, which I had to admit pleased the more flippety-gibbet female audience.

We were a fine team 'til he took up smoking cigarillos. They was a potent mixture of banana skins and Nicaraguan weed, and what with me going through my 'pipe-smoking' phase we couldn't see a damn thing with all that tobacco smoke and steam swirling round.

At one point I was facing the wrong way and Bobby D had fallen out of the DJ box and was lying in a heap on the dancefloor, with a bottle of beer in one hand and a bent cheroot in his mouth, laughin' his silly head off.

Didn't need no dry ice, that's for sure. He was a master of electronics, though and rigged me up all manner of gadgets, including a bubble blowing machine and a massage table.

Great kid, but hated people and could be viciously rude to the customers, and for that reason the Discos didn't really fit in with his lifestyle choices.

And that's when he decided to be a taxi cab driver.

Radio Randy 1971/72

(GET UP I FEEL LIKE BEING A) SEX MACHINE – JAMES BROWN

I KNOW YOU GOT SOUL – BOBBY BYRD

MR. BIG STUFF – JEAN KNIGHT

MEMPHIS SOUL STEW – KING CURTIS

FAMILY AFFAIR – SLY AND THE FAMILY STONE

SUPERSTITION – STEVIE WONDER

GET ON TOP – TIM BUCKLEY

SUPERFLY – CURTIS MAYFIELD

SLICED TOMATOES – JUST BROTHERS

LOVE AND HAPPINESS – AL GREEN

Heart-wrenching vocals and more of a funky feel from some strong acts here. I just wanna let loose with these tracks and get some fat bass slappin' goin' on!

James Brown kicks it all off with his cohort Bobby Byrd taking the Funk on to another level.

Al Green finishes off this particular Top ten with a song just dripping in Soul gravy.

'Hey, come to Carl's coffee bar Bank Street, West Village, man. Smoke some pot, take LSD and have a coffee. You can vomit on the table, don't sweat it…..er……got weed too……go on you deserve it!'

Chapter 7

Mr. Big Stuff

Perhaps the most influential person on my career, after my dear Mama Feelgood and Sly Stone, oh and my Indian cousins, too. And Dolly Parton, was Rico Figaro. Better known today as Disco Dick.

What a guy. Stood six foot six, in his high-heeled sneaker round-toed boots with his skin-tight latex jumpsuits and a mop of jet black afro style hair-do.

He looked like the *Jackson Five* and Cleo Laine's lovechild crossed with the Hair Bear bunch, all three of them. Was he Puerto Rican? Was he Costa Rican? Or was he Manchesterican? Yeah, that's right, he was.

Manchesterican.

From Manchester, England, a great sprawling mess of smog, dampness and filth, but he was very charming and knew his way round a turntable and allowed me booth time when I was washing glasses and dancing at the Catfish Club in Harlem.

I got to know Rico well when I got my first job on my return to the Big Apple in the fall of '74. I quit school and went straight on to the College of life and getting down. Big sis, Loretta had started at this new place, the Catfish, another little sweaty joint in Harlem that her old boss, Ike had opened.

Rico was a British guy, first one I'd ever met, apart from my daddy. His given name was Derek Figg, though he affected the name Rico Figaro, which certainly sounded more exotic and was Latino sounding, which was the current buzz of the times. Ya know, like Carlos Fandango, or Giuseppe Bukkake.

This guy'd always lube up with fake tan, face and neck only, shades and a gold medallion, plus Gola sports towelling socks and underwear, to soak up all the sweat. Classy.

Plain old Derek would have stood out a tad in that place, with his baby blond curls, and beatnik polyester shirts, so his new persona gave him the opportunity to hide behind the glasses.

He'd been some kind of big shot band promoter in the mid 'Sixties, when all these British acts came over to the States. *The Beatles, Rolling Stones, Kinks, Small Faces,* and so on. Those Brits dominated the charts back then and it was a time for a musical revolution. A lot of these acts were taking the Blues, rockin' them up and giving them back to us Americans.

Derek looked after a singer from the northern British clubs named Black Pudding Bertha and also managed a band called *'Danny Stink and the Facemelters'*, who had minor success in the UK having pretended to be the *Stones* on a TV talent show.

Their limited reputation was in tatters so they had to split town. That's when Derek brought them over to New York on the Queen Mary ocean liner, from Southampton, England.

Took them three months and the band where somewhat travel battered, having been stowed away inside one of the lifeboats, hidden under a dirty orange tarp for the whole journey. The tickets were stolen, apparently, according to Derek, as he was walking through the red-light district of Southampton one night. Derby Road was notorious back then as the prostitution capital of England, and Derek should know. He shared his flat with a street-girl back then. She paid him her rent in kind so he was always having cash flow problems.

The band were innocents, all of them under twenty. A bunch of good looking young guys in tight suits and floppy hair. But they had a shipwrecked look as they slipped off the Queen Mary in New York in '67.

Well, they got a gig in a small theatre in Manhattan on arrival, just to try and raise some dough for digs, and were booed off stage. Derek high-tailed it to a girlfriend's place in Harlem and laid low for a while. Another good reason to change names, I guess. Last I heard they was backing Herbie Hancock.

[Author's note – the Facemelters were booked to play a support slot for *Tony* Hancock, the British comedian, but failed to show up for their first gig. Lead singer Danny Stink, (real name Sidney Stink) took a job as a chef on an illegal gambling ship heading to Louisiana, and was eaten by an alligator while using the bathroom in a swamp.]

The Catfish club was bigger than Ike's old place, the Shaking Hand, and he had a faithful following of regulars.

Man, that place swung and I was in the kitchen groovin' and a movin' with Loretta promoted to the kitchen boss and Rico on the wheels of steel. Of course, Disco was still in its infancy then, so cats dug his Soul cuts. I'd pester that dude throughout the night with requests for songs. Songs I knew would get the place swinging, songs I'd heard and that had the groove.

He took me under his great flabby wing 'cos he could see I knew my sounds, and I became his warm-up guy. The Club would close between three and six, Monday thru Thursday. That's when I went up into the pulpit box, where Derek worked his craft, and learnt about all the tools of the trade; how to mix, how to set the mood. And to change gears song-wise, from first to warp-drive.

Then when the place opened up, there was me, little ol' Randy from the other side of the tracks, a honky with a mixed heritage playing the music I loved to a Club full of people from all sides of the tracks.

We'd have office workers, businessmen types, a few hookers, people celebrating, people drowning their sorrows, bachelor parties, bridesmaids and pimps, pushers and Soul-trainers. I guess it was a half black, half white crowd, with the music transcending race and class barriers. They were in the joint for the same reason. Good times and great music and maybe a little chemical assistance. They all knew their music, and it was my kinda music; Soul, Funk, a piece of Latino stylin', the Motown sound, the Atlantic sound.

Occasionally I'd mix it up by dropping in something way off outta the back pocket of my double denim jeans.

One night I was feeling groovy and dropped the needle on Kenny Rogers and *'Just Dropped In, to see what condition my condition was in'*. Totally out of whack, and the Ric-Fig was not amused. But I stood by it, and the crowd dug it.

Another tune off centre was *'I Love to Boogie'* by T-Rex. Had a great upbeat tempo and you could slide the volume way up on the intro beat. This mixed in well with a lot of Soul stompers too, like *'Nutbush City Limits'* by Tina Turner. I remember *'Rebel Rebel'* being a club favourite too, with the white soul boys.

I defended my right to play what I wanted and not be restricted by a *Musical Policy*, whatever the hell that is. Ike seemed to dig it and the Club was busting at the seams.

Come 1975 I was on my own. Rico had split after an incident involving a soul singer and a lemon. The scandal hit town, and Rico had to lay low. We was attracting a more mixed audience by now. More whites and Italians, some hippies even.

But Rico was a player. He could see the whole Disco thing erupting and he was an entrepreneur; wheelin' and dealin' to catch him a fat slice o' the pie, with lemon.

He became Disco Dick, dyed his baby blond curly locks jet black this time, rather than mid-brown and teased it all up into an enormous Afro; donned his crazy outfits and hit the decks at the Funky Eel Club on 49th street.

Ike's Catfish club was now my milky domain and didn't I just lay back and suckle on its teats. I was seventeen and on the scene, gettin' down just for the funk of it. It was the perfect time, music-wise to be in the City, laying down some fine grooves and bustin' my moves.

Then came the Copacabana scandal. Which was only a scandal after that blabbermouth Barry Manilow wrote his damn song in 1978.

Really, it was a simple tale of love and loss and lust.

I had my own club by now, The Electric Lady Garden, 5th Avenue and 52nd Street. It was a ponderous afternoon and I'd been unwinding by performing some stretching exercises to a *Jacksons* record. My personal masseur, Leroy Fontaine was giving the back of my legs a rub down with some oil and apricot balm.

Just Then Rico came upstairs to my personal suite. It was 1976 and Rico/Dick was once again back on the scene. Mud only stuck for a little while in the Big Apple back then. Same as now, I guess. I admonished Dick for busting in on me unannounced. Now Dick's are prone to do that sometimes, ladies, when they're gettin' a little excitable and frisky. I recommend a short sharp slap on the head. Show them who's boss.

I dismissed Leroy, took a shower and we went downstairs to the club to blow the froth off a couple of beers.

We got to talking about chicks, as guys do and I happened to mention this dancer friend of mine who was hot, and more importantly, single. Rico/Dick was instantly on the alert. Again, excitable, and I resisted the temptation to slap his fat cheeks. His afro was like a massive black halo and I didn't want to upset its seemingly fragile balance.

Violence having been averted, I went to change out of my silk and chiffon shower robe, and into something a little less comfortable and off we headed to East 60th Street. Dick was like a hunting hound, sniffing out the prey.

The Copacabana had just reopened, capitalising on the Disco movement and was highly decadent. Potted palms and plants decorated the whole of the main room with Brazilian themed uniforms for the Bartenders and a real tropical feel throughout the place, including colourful birds of paradise. You gotta love a parrot, right? Right on.

You know the story. Lola the showgirl, up on the stage shimmying to a quiet crowd that's in that early evening.

After her dance, Lola spots me and just beams the brightest whitest smile, takes off her fruit bowl hat and sashays over to where me and Rico was sitting. Which happened to be at a table on the edge of the dancefloor, with a bucket of Champagne on ice and a plate of chilli nachos and pickled cucumbers. Olives on the side.

Lola was all woman with curves that seemed to go on indefinitely. She had that classic 'fifties screen goddess figure, like Jane Russell or Marilyn Monroe. Those languid eyes drew you in like a cougar prowling round its prey. Not my type, a might too direct in a fierce kinda way, although I could appreciate the female form.

But Rico had his mouth open and saliva and guacamole was pooling around his lower lip like pea soup. He let out a whistle of admiration, with difficulty and we all had to dry ourselves off with some linen napkins and a finger bowl.

I paid particular attention to the open neck of Lola's gown, slipping my hand in to worry her hardening rose buds, whilst Rico took the opportunity to caress her naked thigh. Lola laughed, and, well you know the rest. The bartender, some Italian small time hoodlum, Tony, just couldn't stand this blatant erotic tension any longer.

He too, had been ogling the girl and was sore that she'd turned down his advances ever since the Club had reopened. Whatta schmuck.

He vaulted the bar and dived into Rico with his fists pounding into his soft belly. The table and chairs went crashing to the floor as I leapt to smother Lola and protect her from the animalistic brawl. She was squirming underneath me, as the battle raged next to us. After a while, the wriggling became more urgent, and I realised she was trying to make out. Time and a place, lady. Time and a place! I guess it was my own fault, still having hold of a gherkin.

Anyway, all this rumpus was bound to attract the cops, so I took my small Derringer from a holster strapped to my lower leg, still trying to grapple with Lola and passed it to Rico to frighten the kid into quitting.

'Show him the piece, man', I said. 'Just don't let it go off too early', (this was to Lola)

'Aaaarghhh', yelled Rico and aimed the gun.

'Ohhhhhhh', went Lola and went all shivery and limp against me. Everything seemed to grind down into slow motion as Rico squeezed the trigger.

Then it all sped up again with the sound of the pistol shot. Lola screamed, Rico fainted and I had to drop my shoulder in to him. Dang, it was like trying to move a truck. So, I summoned up a fast, satanic incantation and slowly there was movement. Dick broke wind, allowing me to get a proper purchase. Slowly I managed to brace my knees and lifted this great lifeless sack of British meat and potatoes up and over my back. Damn him and his curries and late night snacking. And damn the hell outta me for getting inappropriately horny as I wrestled my pants back up one handed and stuck the distressed gherkin into the side of my mouth, Clint Eastwood style.

I staggered once to get my balance and then lent forward to barge our way out of the joint lickety split.

Just in the nick o' time, as it transpired, for as we turned the corner the sirens were wailing louder and louder. I hailed a cab and we retired back to the Lady Garden to assess the damage.

My back and shoulders were on fire, with carrying a giant Golliwog around town, so I'd have to get Leroy to give me a rub down, for sure. My silk blouse was all rucked up to hell, and the pickled vegetable was in tatters.

I called up my cop friend, Kowalski that evening to find out the skinny. Tony was alive, but in a lot of pain. Rico had managed to shoot him in the groin. Oooh, nasty. But not bad considering he'd shot with his eyes closed. And besides, the sucker deserved it. It also transpired that he was wanted by the cops on several counts of stealing decorative rubber plant trees.

The cops were happy, Lola was passed out in an ecstatic swoon and the manager of the Copa was delighted, because as it turned out, Tony had been skimming the cash register. And Rico was safe which was all I really cared about. We could all relax and sleep safe in our beds, away from the hustlers, cops, crazy lust-hungry fruit bats and guns.

It all seemed to have settled down, 'til I found out the very next day that Lola had a crazy crush on me. She came mooning round to the Garden, sucking on a straw all suggestive like. She didn't even have a drink at the time.

Well, I knew just what to do to make amends. I got Rico to woo her. He owed me one and I ain't partial to being stalked around the City by some half crazed jizz-junkie, fruit basket who can't keep her brassiere on. Not this one anyway. Once was enough, and any more than that and you got a relationship situation going on. Much harder to ejaculate oneself from that in a hurry.

So, Rico had his mission. He had to make Lola fall in love with him. He just loved a challenge and threw himself into the task ahead. And he didn't seem to mind about sloppy seconds. And a week later that big haired Soul cat had pulled it off. I was off the hook and free to gallivant without peaking over my shoulder, looking out for a tropical straw hat heading my way.

But now, of course, Rico was a marked man. He'd made his soft peach bed, and now he was slipping and sliding and rolling around in it, sapped of all his vital juices and vitamins. But there was no escape plan, like a window or a fast horse. He was trapped in the love hungry warm embrace of a nympho clam, sucking the very life outta him.

I had to feel sorry for the dude, he couldn't exactly blend. That's when I came up with the idea of a world tour, to England.

Rico Figg, or now Disco Dick as he was, couldn't go through another name change. Though we did toy with the idea. He fancied becoming a Private Eye, Jack Spanner.

'What we need Dick Figarino', (even I was getting confused as to who he really was. And I'd invented his Dick name.)

'What we need is a plan, man.'

'You crazy fool, Randy. I ain't got no time for no plan, man. That bitch is gonna rip off my vitals. She told me she would, if I ever left her, 'n I believe her. Other day she was cupping me and slicing her teeth over 'em, saying "your balls are mine, Dick. They'll make nice earrings." You gotta help me, Randy, man. I'm rather attached to my bojangles.'

61

'No sweat Diggedy Figg, I can feel your pain.'

I was actually slightly distracted by the thought of Lola's inventive techniques and wondered if I shouldn't pay her one more visit. Old time's sake. Using her teeth? Sounded kinda exhilarating...making me feel .....somewhat......

'Randy, *RANDY*', Dick brought me out of my daydreamin'.

'Cool it, man. I got it.' And indeed, I had. A plan. A rather clever one, too, even if'n I do say so myself. Which I do, and did. My plan ticked all the boxes allowing the Rickster to keep his dignity, and his danglys.

'Oh, man I is toast with the middle bit all cut out.'

'Quit snivelling, man, you're getting all salty tears all over my cashmere hot pants. Now listen up. Disco is hot right now, you dig. The people, they just can't get enough o' that Disco, Funk and stuff. All you gotta do is lay low here at the Lady Garden for a couple o' days, 'til we can get you out of Dodge. Then we is gonna get you on a fast plane or a slow boat and go on a world tour.

'A world what now? What you say, Randy man?

'A world tour of the UK', I said emphatically

'A tour of the...Randy, you just about lost your mind? I can't go back to England. I'd be better off takin' my chances with Lola the Steamroller.'

'No no, it's totally cool Figaro, daddy-o. You are a new person. You are not Derek Figg no more, man. You've even lost your accent. You speak normal, just like me, brother. I got me a dude in Hell's Kitchen who can rustle y'up a new passport and everything. It's all settled.

'Where am I going?'

'My old Daddy's working a club over in London and he can get you a weekly shindig, then you can work on creating a buzz and you're on your way.'

Rico/Dick was a little down beat but he was brightening to the idea and we worked on the detail into the night over a Pina Colada with Cherry sorbet and Fanta, two backing singers from the Club.

Dick had a little catchphrase he used in those days,

"Rockin' the Disco across the nation with bigger platforms than Grand Central Station." Whatta man, whatta man, what a mighty good man. And what a line. But, of course that sounded too American, in my mind. Quick as a flash Dick intercedes.

'Let's change it to *"He's got the style, he's got the gumption, with bigger platforms than Clapham Junction."*

'Hmm'. I pondered this a-whiles. I knew a little of the U.K. having distant cousins there, so knew I could help with the promotional ideas.

'Hey Dick, you know the Brits, they don't really dig the word "gumption", it's like, Shakespearean to them dudes. You might as well say 'my gramophone has a nice tone'. Try using "spunk", instead.'

Well, it turned out there was a communication breakdown at the printers in England, and Dick's tour kinda got bogged down with a less than flattering marketing angle.

"He's got the spunk, he's got the lotion. He's covering the whole of Clapham Junction."

The tour didn't go too well for him, as I recall. He had to ditch his leaflets and posters and survive on word of mouth.

Disco Dick played all over the South of England throughout 1976. I'd get regular postcards from Southampton, Plymouth, Bournemouth, Brighton, Newport Pagnell. He was living the dream like a cat who's loving the cream. Milking and kicking out the jams, mother rocker.

Like I said, whatta man. And it was almost like the band *Brotherhood of Man* wrote their big song, *'Figaro'* about him. A big hit in Europe and gave me and the boys a chuckle.

I told Barry Manilow this little tale, (but leaving out the bit about the gherkin,) over spiced rum and bar snacks at Captain Ahab's Whale Shack down on Beekman Street, and the next I knew, Barry goes off and knocks off his little song and the whole world knows the sorry saga. And not a penny did I make, damn that Manilow shark. And I lent him the dollar tip, too. He did stump up the bar tab, though, so I'm not too down on the dude. Just don't get me started on the making of *'Mandy'*. She was a hot one, too.

Lola continued working at the Copacabana and gained a little popularity 'til she finally met a billionaire Church man and married him. In her yellow dress with fruit basket headdress, so I'm told.

I ain't one to judge, and I have total respect for all the religions of the world; Hindu, Buddhism, Shinto, Vegetarianism and Rastafarian. But Christianity has some strange parameters. I'm God-fearin', for sure. But my religion is in my heart. Don't need to be actually attending no brick-built Church and go banging my breast or trying to stay awake. But I'll make the right noises while still keeping an interested eye on the ladies of the parish, in their tight summer dresses. All busting out like buds in the springtime.

Yep, you can keep your church for someone who digs that action. Besides, the beer's watered down and there's only one wine, 'nuff said. And pass the cocktail menu there, fly guy.

Radio Randy 1973

THINK (ABOUT IT) – LYN COLLINS

GET ON THE GOOD FOOT – JAMES BROWN

HIGHER GROUND – STEVIE WONDER

HERE I AM – AL GREEN

LONG TRAIN RUNNING – THE DOOBIE BROTHERS

SO MUCH TROUBLE – SIR JOE QUARTERMAIN

JUNGLE BOOGIE – KOOL AND THE GANG

LAW OF THE LAND – THE TEMPTATIONS

YOU DID IT – ANN ROBINSON

LIVING FOR THE CITY – STEVIE WONDER

Ah, Lyn Collins. Another chick from the James Brown stable, though she ain't no horse. Does like apples however. In fact, one of her songs, 'Mama Feelgood' was inspired by mah dear ol' mama after James wanted to get his band into shape for an upcoming tour and sent them all round to the Feelgood homestead for some positive energy and oily back rubs.

Stevie's got two tracks here. In my opinion his finest records.

'Co-ordination is a way of life for the DAKS wearer. We got over 20 shades of beige, caramel and cavalry twill in our DAKS trouser range alone. All in good quality synthetic wool. Get yours at Wanamaker's.

Chapter 8

Dance Across the floor

Whatever kind of music you're into, it's gotta move you, physically, unless you're dead, or at a funeral, or both. So, don't just stand there dude and dudess, shake what your mama gave ya!

And as Hamilton Bohannon once told me,

'Randy, it's not a question of getting' down, but actually how low you can go.' Yeah, I'm digging that action. Giving me soul satisfaction, Ham-Bo.

But that's not really appropriate behind a DJ Booth, unless you're tying a shoelace or picking up a piece of discarded lingerie.

Therefore, if you're going to dance you need to be situated next to a stage, or on it. From purpose-built discotheques, to refurbished ballrooms, smoky juke joints to high class casinos, most places will have a stage on which to *"Get up, stand up, strut your funky stuff, sho' nuff"*.

So, set the needle in the groove, and you're ready to move.

There were so many dance crazes, during the 'Seventies in particular. We had the *'the Bump'*, 'the funky chicken', 'the robot', 'the lawnmower', 'the sprinkler', and one of my favourites, 'the wheelbarrow.' There was also *'the Hustle'*. This was very popular but, as with all instrumentals, became all about being seen and doing your thang. Mighty disconcerting if you're the DJ, as you want people looking at *you*.

I much preferred *'the Spanish Hustle'* anyways, by the Fatback Band. Oh, Truck Turner those guys knew how to raise hell in a handcart with a funky beat.

I was always dancing to any song and I liked to do a little thing called the Randy shuffle, which became quite the movement of the moment, filling the bridge between *'the Bump', 'the Hustle'* and the *'Oops upside your head'* boating dance craze.

Now I could never see the point of that move as it only resulted in a dirty beer stain on the seat of your satin pants and the undignified bit when all the boat rockers and human oar-ravers had to get up at the end, tucking themselves in and trying to look cool for the next dance. Yeah, sure, it was certainly a way to grab the love handles, and more, of the person in front of you, if you couldn't wait for the slowies. But fraught with hazards, like where to put your champagne flute, or beret.

Anyway, I invented the Randy shuffle after an ice cube became trapped under one of my Cuban heels one night during an energetic routine to *'Move on up'* by Curtis Mayfield. It was 1976, as I recall, and I was at the Electric Coconut club, up on the stage with the Kaytel sisters, Kay and Tel, couple of mighty fine pulsating dancers.

It was during the bongo bit and my feet just kinda slipped as I pivoted on a 180-degree arc across the stage, my scarlet red satin shirt with bolero sleeves swinging out in a windmill configuration as my legs became a blur, trying to get a grip on the slippery stage.

At the break of the song, my percussion amigo, Bingo Bongo Basil kept the jungle rhythms pounding. His great hammy hands skipped over the Bongo skins while I hip-dropped with a half turn to step behind the booth to allow the club to go on a drum trip before slapping on *'I Don't Need No Doctor'* by Ray Charles.

Basil worked his hard fingers across the skins while I dug Ray's voice. That dude had more Soul than he could control and became a very good friend of mine, who I got to know personally while working on the 'Blues Brothers' movie. I didn't need a doctor, but I required a whiskey.

It was a seamless mix as Curtis went on one of his rhythmic jams, and I mixed Ray in over the top of Curtis and Basil on a percussive freight train. The audience went wild and Kay & Tel (I could never remember which was which) snaked into the booth with me for some bumpin' and grindin' and sweet lovin' from behindin'.

That one piece of timing created a phenomenon. The dancing, that is, not the romancing, which is another story.

Now, little did I know, that my accidental hot shoe shuffle had created a craze. Even Muhammed Ali came around the next afternoon, begging me to teach him.

I was in the Marabou Bar across the street from the club, having me some siesta time, enjoying a breakfast cocktail of Sangria with Sambuca and Daiquiri, couple o' cocktail waitresses I was helping make a pop record with.

Ali comes in and squeezes his mighty and perfect frame at a booth with a couple of his guys in suits. I could see he was itching; itching to talk to me. I had on my fiery red silk kimono with various gallivanting dragons kicking up a helluva racket all over it, and my customary Yves Saint Laurent over-sized tinted sunglasses with big lenses.

Eventually, over he comes, gliding like a panther between the scattered bean bags.

'Randy, you gotta teach me that thing.' He said with his satin smooth voice.

'Yo! What's up my main man Mo-man, cousin Cassius. What thang?'

Ali looked at me with that glint in his eye.

'You know' he said, 'that shuffle you pulled last night at the Coconut.'

'Hey man', I said, playing it cool. 'Just a little crazy step I been a-working on, and besides, you got the moves already, with the whole butterfly floating thing and the Ali shuffle and the shoulder drop!'

He reached across. *('Forward'*, I thought) and took a sip of my cocktail. I let it slide.

'Yeah, but I'm getting old and everyone knows the Ali shuffle, I need something fresh. I gotta up my game. Teach me, will you Randy?'

Then he looked whimsically over at Sambuca and Daiquiri draped over my chaise-longue in the corner, looking all seductively semi-dressed and fine. I let that go too; he was appreciating the female form and the man had taste.

'You know the dance is won far away from witnesses – behind the lines, in the gym, long before I fight under those lights.'

'Ain't that the truth, brother.' I said, but inwardly confused.

But, you know, I appreciated the man's candour. And I had enormous respect for the guy and what he stood for. So, while I went 'n changed into my dancing pants, Ali stripped down to his silk boxing shorts. He never left home without them apparently, although that high waist will play havoc with the drop of the shirt, so I would not recommend it.

We sparred a little, all joshing like. I had one of the girls line up my *Earth, Wind and Fire* album, *'Gratitude'* and away we went, boppin' and twistin', dancin' and cavortin'. He was a quick learner and thanked me, too hard; crushing the diamante ring on my right hand as he pumped it mercilessly.

'Hey, no sweat Champ, go get 'em.'

Mr. Ali had not actually broken sweat at all and left with his flunkeys in tow, looking somewhat bemused. Meanwhile Ali seemed to be walking taller and with a springier step. What a champ, and what a gent.

Now while this was all cooking, I had espied the bouncer of the Coconut lurking in the corner of the joint. He kinda came with the club, you know, like:

'Settees, carpet, lights, oh and Big Fast Eddie ….'

'Hmm, say what?'

'I said "settees, drapes,"' says the legal guy with the glasses and badly fitted suit. Pitiful. We was getting down to business, when I was taking over the club a few months earlier.

'Hold on, Mr. Sack O'Potatoes. Who's Big Fat Hetty? I don't wanna bomp no more, wi' no big fat woman, daddy-o!'

'Er, yes Mr. Feelgood. The Coconut Club comes with all fixtures, fittings and one Mr. Edward Crump as part of the Sale agreement. It's in the contract, I'm afraid.'

Well, cut a long and tedious story short; like I said, part of the fixtures and fittings. A hulking great brute of a man, who liked his club door how he liked his women; square with an out-sized hessian mat out front.

He was an amateur boxer too. Which was handy as a deterrent, front of house. He had great scarred, meaty hands, with fingers so big, I swear moulds were taken of them, to be sold in the sex shops along West Village. Or so my friend Mandy Pussycat once told me, over a vigorous game of squash one day, which ended when we got too hot for clothes, and retired naked to the shower block.

So, of course, Fat Eddie had seen Ali come in and wanted a piece of the action.

In those days, a lot of boxers had a handle, a moniker, like *"Sugar Ray"*, or *"Smokin'"*, or *"the Brown Bomber"*. Well Eddie wanted a new angle to make up for the fact that he spent more time sitting on the canvas than on his damned stool.

He went by *'Big Fast Dancing Eddie "the Dump" Crump'*. Bit of a mouthful, you could say. Much like his fingers.

His theory was that he would have an enormous evacuation of his bowels just before a fight, thus getting him down to his fightin' weight, and to be lighter on his toes. And to prove this, he'd scuttle off to the men's room, knees slightly bent and sweat poppin' out of his furrowed brow. Then you'd hear an animalistic grunt as he closed the cubicle door, and laid a couple o' King Kong's fingers in the john. Once he'd done his business, he was ready to jig around in the ring, poppin' and jivin' all over and doing little flippety skips.

'Hey Hoss', he was talking to me now. Big fan of the cowboy show, Bonanza.

'Er, hey Hoss. Could you, er, show me some o' dem moves you laid on Mr. Ali, now, just a minute?'

'What the whaaa! You want me to show you the same thing as the Champ! Lord a mercy Eddie! I just this minute sat down.'

'Ah, please, Hoss. I is fightin' Thomas "de Tank" Johnson next week', and his bottom lip started to wobble, so he had me agreeing, the sap. So off he goes and returns from the washroom waddling away in his under crackers.

Oh, sweet sugar dumpling, you ain't never seen nothing like it. A more rancid, grey piece of raggedy ol' filthy garment, had I done never seen, that even a flea scratching street bum would've averted his eyes, not since I was at Woodstock, anyway. I said nothing, well you wouldn't, would you; not wanting to upset a heavyweight Boxing phenomenon, you dig?

Well, over the next few hours I taught him all my moves, and some I didn't even know I had! He was a slow learner and the elastic on his donkey droppers was having a tough job keeping everything together, and a couple of times I had to halt the sparring.

'Hey Champ, your two prize fighters are slugging it out through the ropes again!' I warned him. Of course, I couldn't really be sure if'n he'd popped a couple o' nuggets out with all the exertion. But his great brown wrecking balls were swinging and clackety-clacking all over the place, knocking the great lumbering oaf off balance, and into the furniture.

We broke for iced tea around 4 o'clock, then continued on into the evening. By now 'the Dump' was on his knees, along with his gonads. His underpants were held up with one of my old paisley cravats, mainly to preserve his dignity, but also to stop me losing my luncheon all over the carpet.

And there I stood, berating him with good cheer, and watching him swinging around like a mountain gorilla in a tutu. He got it in the end. Hell, it was only a simple little grapevine thing that he could memorise and we said our goodbyes; him slippin' out the back door and me without a neck tie.

'Keep the cravat' I insisted, as he tried to return it.

It was pleasing to see him taunt opponents with it in the ring. That and his new improved, Randy inspired 'Dump shuffle.'

Another little thing I was doing back then was the 'Buzz'. It was an odd sliding kinda move that Cab Calloway showed me during the shooting of 'the Blues Brothers'. It was like a slow and easy, walking backwards in slow motion, type thing. In fact, I was teaching it to John Belushi one afternoon when Michael Jackson happened by my trailer.

'What ya doin' there Randy', Michael said in his quiet little voice.

'Hey, MJ, check this out', and I popped and toe-slided backwards, with Michael going crazy and clapping his hands.

'Oh, it's like you're weightless. Like you're walking on the moon.' Yeah, and that's how Michael turned that little dance move into the worldwide step called the 'Moonwalk'.

That was the time when I met my hero, Mr. Ray Charles.

'You should never meet your heroes.' Was something Brian Jones once told me as a kid. Ma was a big *Stones* fan and I remember meeting this quiet blond dude with soulful eyes. We were in Muscle Shoals, the recording studio. And ma was laying down some backing vocals. Brian came in and hung out and I guess I'll pin mama down to get the full story on *that,* one of these days.

But anyways, Brian had been left somewhat underwhelmed meeting his own hero, Chuck Berry when the *Stones* came over to the States, early '60s.

'Who do you dig, little fella?' Brian said to me through the fuggy haze of cigarette smoke that was hanging and drifting in the booth. He was picking out some notes on his unplugged electric guitar as Mama was ripping the bejeezus out of some backing vocals in the studio at the time.

'Oh, you know, man. Usual dudes; Otis, Marvin, Etta. And your band's pretty cool too, cat.

'Have you heard of Chuck Berry?' Then he kinda drifted in to his own reverie while a melancholy seemed to sweep across his eyes.

'He was my hero. I was quite sad after meeting him.'

Well, old Chuck could be a pernickety ol' cranky bastardo with some folks. Maybe he was having a bad shirt day. But my motto is "speak as I find", and I loved ol' Chuck. Never met him, mind. But talk about dance moves. Chuck's guitar-toting duck walk just 'bout inspired some of the best axe men ever to spread their legs on a stage. Angus Young for one. Though that short trousered rocker took it to 11 and beyond.

But I did meet my hero, Ray Charles and it was one of my most treasured experiences, alongside sharing a heated pool with the cast of 'Baywatch'. Not really related to this here particular yarn, and you'll find it all set down in my *'Tales from the movies'* recollections.

Getting back to my current tale, I had a lot of time for Michael in those days. He was a shy boy who liked to hang around other celebrities, like myself. Made him feel comfortable.

'I prefer just being with people I like. That's my way of celebrating.' He used to say, 'specially when he was hanging out at the Paradise, getting fondled by the cougars. Those more mature actresses and dancers just loved running their painted talons through Michael's juvenile afro and slipping their hands under his shirt and breathing sweet dirty Jezebel somethings in his soft velvety ear. That's why all the famous faces liked to hang out at the Paradise in those hedonistic times. No one was there to judge, just to have a good time. Livin' easy, lovin' free. And that's why Michael had a satisfied grin, more often than not, with his shirt untucked, lipstick on his lobes and happy languid eyes on the faces of those sharing his seat.

In many ways, MJ had a childlike innocence and an eagerness to please. But there was a seriousness there too, which was reflected in some of his lyrics. Opposite of me, but we complemented each other, like I was the ying and he was the yang;

I was the toast, and he was the marmalade, or beans. We centred each other. Terrific dancer too, and we'd swap dance moves and lines for songs.

David Hodo was another fine dancer. Better known as the construction guy from the *Village People*, David used to dance his tight-fitting vest off at the Coconut Club in '77. I dug his style as did the chicks. He never really took advantage of this, much. Don't know why, just happy to dance I guess. And I was always happy to take the ladies on his behalf.

It was about this time I got a small part, on David's recommendation, in a Broadway production of *Albert and Louise,* produced by the failed magician and bit part actor Rodney Van Spankkir and directed by Howard Daniels. Somehow, they managed to get Deborah White over from England. She was hot property just then, like Diana Rigg or Raquel Welch. But she agreed to the gig even though Rodney was a virtual unknown. He did, however, have a young, mostly male cast. And that's what swung it for Ms. White.

We was made to line up at the theatre, back stage after a couple of weeks' rehearsal to receive her majesty, Lady Deborah. In she glided, like an Egyptian queen assessing the troops. What we didn't know, as we stood to attention, in our figure hugging Farah's and sweaty T-shirts was she really was checking us out. She was in town and looking for a fun time.

It was instant love at first sight for me. Well more like horn at first sight. She was a goddess. A classic beauty, oozing sexuality, dressed casually but seductively in tight leather pants, like Emma Peel, with pixie boots and a poncho. Her dark hair glistening like a crystal silk waterfall wherever she walked. I wasn't yet ready for that kind of sophistication and with some gentle persuasion and manoeuvring, I lined up my pal, Brian Garcia as her beau. Besides I was a free bird just then, and didn't want to upset the show, you dig. Not to mention upsetting two erotic dancers at *Cynthia's*

House, a basement club just east of central Park. Or Cynthia for that matter.....

As it turned out Brian lasted but the one night, while I hid in the wardrobe, watching.

Hey, don't judge me. Women have a way of identifying my weakness, and then exploiting me.

Brian was so nervous he made the mistake of coming to Ms. White's hotel bed the first night still wearing his underwear. It would have been easily dealt with except he was sporting a silk corset to hold his belly in. I felt a little guilty as I'd acquired it for him from Mandy (remember her?) at her exotic emporium. But the dang fool accessorized with peek-a-boo panties to match. It was a car crash of a night for Brian, despite Deborah retaining her composure (having fallen outta bed laughing). But Brian was so upset and could not rise to the occasion, even with Deborah's skilful Jazz trumpeting, and scuttled out of the room.

Luckily, I had found a second wind. What was I supposed to do?

So, me and David Hodo, as I mentioned, had the same physique and hairstyle and tight trousers and people thought we was brothers. In a way, we were. I got a small part in his band's movie, *'You can't stop the music'*, dancing and getting down. We was two cats from the same alley and we even took each other's place at red carpet shindigs. Rest of the guys never knew, but we found it a helluva gas.

Just two regular guys swapping gigs, Broadway gossip and hats.

ROCK YOUR BABY – GEORGE MCCRAE

CROSS THE TRACKS – MACEO AND THE MACKS

IN THE BOTTLE – GIL SCOTT HERON

PICK UP THE PIECES – AVERAGE WHITE BAND

HANG ON IN THERE BABY – JOHNNY BRISTOL

LADY MARMALADE – LABELLE

ROCK THE BOAT – HUES CORPORATION

EXPANSIONS – LONNIE LISTON SMITH

YOU'RE THE FIRST, MY LAST, MY EVERYTHING – BARRY WHITE

SOUL POWER '74 – MACEO AND THE MACKS

Widely acknowledged as the first ever Disco record, 'Rock Your Baby' has that "tee, tick a tee, tick a tee, tick a tee" hi-hat I was mentioning. This gives it a bit of an urgent forward momentum. Some records will replicate this kind of beat with a tambourine. But listen to *KC and the Sunshine Band's 'That's the way I like it'*. That is the very definition of a Disco sound. It has all the ingredients. I can't believe I didn't include it in this here top ten. I need to go to one of them Russian saunas and get beaten by Mistress Olga with a sprig of a birch tree for that omission.

And then there's some other early cuts along the same lines. Very influential on the scene; together with some fine pieces of funk mastery. Butter me up sugar, 'cos I'm a-wantin' mah toast!

'In the Bottle' has got to be one of those tunes you could squeeze in today, even, and you'll get a real groove on. Gotta watch out for that beginning there, when Gil counts it in. I liked to loop this when mixing into *'Shame, Shame, Shame'*. Weren't no shame for me, I just love this jazzy cut.

I think Funk just about hit the towering inferno with some of these fat slabs of Bass slappin' monsters. And Patti Labelle and her band got all silvery in their sexy space outfits. Point of fact, the space theme kept re-emerging throughout the Disco decade.

I've still got my knee-high silver boots from a *Kool and the Gang* show I did.

Chapter 9

Native New Yorker

For me, my musical enlightenment began with a quest.

I was always tippy, tippy, tapping out the beats from the radio or record player on anything I could touch with my searching fingers; pencils on desks at school, or kitchen cutlery at home. I near enough drove ma poor dotin' mother half-crazy with the sounds of my percussion, not to mention my dancin' feet. But I am gonna mention that too.

Now, my ma brung us four kids up alone after my daddy hopped on a ship one day to head back to England, his mother country.

He was a mean son of a gun, and ma had just about had enough of his shines. He was either out all day and night, up to who knows what, or kicking round the front porch drinking whiskey and getting under mama's feet.

One day he said to her,

'Well now, there's a strook o' luck so it is, mother Feelgood. Me pals, Willie and Doogie has got us all some work, starting in the mahning, droiving Christmas trees down to Virginia, cash on the barrel, so it is. Hee hee! Oi feels loik a noight out so I do. Get your coat on woman.'

'Oh my, where we going, Donny?' Said Ma, all excited.

'Nowhere' he said, Oi'm turning off de heating. Hee hee.' Well that was the last straw, and thirty minutes later ma had slung out a sack with Pa's clothes and belongings on to the front yard. It was just one of Daddy's little jokes. But in truth I think she was getting' tired of his *'tree fellas'* routines and wanted to head up to New York away from the heat and the flies of Alabama.

The Feelgood family was a blend of half Irish, half Cherokee, half Negro slave with a half Latino thrown in for good measure. I was twice the man I oughta be, and consequently we had kith and kin scattered across the 50 states and beyond.

We moved to Brooklyn when I was just a skinny little lad and I quickly felt right at home in the vibrancy of the big city. I blossomed from street kid to street-wise kid and took all aspects of my education seriously; from Math to English and Dance classes and Social History.

Mama had a serious face on, one afternoon, as I arrived home from school, and I knew there was some black cloud looming around the kitchen, as I stepped across the front step.

'Randy' she hollered. Always could project her voice, my mama. 'Randy, you've been dancing and boogieing and a-shimmying all your life, and it's gotten so bad that your sister broke wind in the bathtub last week and you started to toe tap a rhythm. Now, I'm not telling you to stop, cos I can see you're taken with the music, just like I was many years ago, when my hips were thinner and my bosom was higher. But, oh lordy, you're wearing holes in my linoleum and the porch is sagging! Much the same as yo' poor mother is!'

'Now, I know you got the music in you my son, so I is gonna send you to see a cousin of mine, way out west. Now go pack a bag, cos you is leaving in the morning on the Greyhound.'

'Out west?' I said, somewhat alarmed.'

'Mm, hmm. You're bright Randy. You done your schoolin', but there's life lessons I can't teach ya. Your daddy done left us all when you was a itty bitty child and there's a whole world out there for you to explore.' She was weepin' now, huge fat tears slidin' down her chubby brown cheeks as she wrestled me to her breast and crushed me in a lovin' embrace.

'Now go on. Mama loves ya but it's time to fly the nest. But come back, ya hear.' And off she went, blubbing again.

I didn't know what to think. I was fluttering with a mixture of excitement, fear, anticipation and trepidation, like a Jambalaya of jumbled emotions as I grabbed one of my daddy's old duffle bags from under my bed and packed my things.

'We'll have dinner tonight, then my friend Sylvester 'll pick you up after breakfast', Ma hollered, gentle-like, from the kitchen.

That evening the five of us ate and reminisced about old times and laughed and played word games and laughed some more.

I woke up next morning with optimistic anxiety. It was an odd feeling as I stretched and got dressed and looked around my bedroom, with my treasured baseball pendant, and pictures of football stars and singers stuck on the wall. I was a kid still, but somehow, stepping through the door I felt I was becoming a man.

Breakfast, when I finally emerged from my room, consisted of a feast Mama had prepared for the big event. She had a voracious appetite, that lady and had cooked up a banquet for the family, and also friends and neighbours who she'd invited to drop by to see me off.

There were eggs, grits, great piles of bacon with toast and biscuits and tall jugs of juice and iced tea. I smelled some creole dishes too, cooling on the window sill, and someone was stirring chilli.

Sly pulled up in his cherry red, creating a stir amongst the kids from the block. He tossed a few pennies to a bunch of them to keep an eye on his wheels as he hopped over the railings to our porch. Why he didn't use the steps I couldn't figure.

Ma wrapped her massive arms around him and near suffocated him, as she crushed him to her breast in a bear hug. He managed to pop out with his shades all askew and the feather in his hair all crushed, and bits of biscuit squashed onto his face from Ma's cleavage crumbs. But ma squeezed his cheeks and kissed 'em clean. Disgusting woman.

Sylvester went by the handle Sly, and him and his band, *'Sly and the Family Stone'* had just performed at Madison Square Garden.

He would often pop by the neighbourhood from time to time, and I always called him Mr. Stone. He was a strange dude but very respectful to Mama Feelgood and us kids. Ma had looked after him at Woodstock back in the day, evidently; taking care of his hair and clothes and personal relaxation. And they'd kept in touch ever since.

Sly seemed to feel some kind of unspoken responsibility towards Mama, and he would come over from time to time, helping us out when he could, despite the fact, as I later found out, his band was fracturing around him.

In fact, Ma used to have a lot of visitors after Pa left, to take advantage of her unique relaxation and therapeutic massaging capabilities.

'Magic hands', guys would say as they stumbled out the back door, all relaxed to hell and back. Ladies too sometimes.

I had my clothes, comb and washbag and whatnot, all crammed in my bag as I sat in the kitchen after breakfast getting' somewhat excited, but also a little sad to be leaving my loving family behind. I'd also packed a few of Sly's old hand-me-downs. He was the most colourful dude I ever knew and he had laid a big bag of clothes on me the previous year on a promotional visit and now I was nearly full grown, some of these duds actually fit me.

I was the strutting peacock on the loose with my homeys from the 'hood, that previous summer in '73. We were the soul brothers, with the swagger and height to look nineteen or twenty when we were barely sixteen.

Me, and Swanny, Dan the man and Reggie the camel. We'd be out ripping up the Lower East side on a Friday and Saturday night getting up to all manner of nocturnal adventures and creeping in at dawn before the family was up. 'Course that area was downright dangerous at night, back then. Muggers, and junkies, alcoholics and guys who'd knife you for a buck. Just so as they could score some dope.

There was a lot of bums and sub-human zombie types, with bad hair and long soiled coats, all shivering round fires lit in old trash bins, just to stay warm. But that's where you'd find the cool bars and shebeens catering for every taste. There was one place I heard of where dudes would go and beat each other, or stick clamps on their privates. One nut I heard tell of, would run a cheese grater over his scrotum. And take a spatula to his John Thomas. I'll not be recommending *that* joint for fine dining.

Dangerous times. So you see, us dudes had to stick together, and no-one was left behind. Army rules. The *'Shakin' Hand'* was a favourite haunt, if you could sneak in, undetected. So, to have Sly's old cast-offs had us looking all hunky dory for funk 'n glory, and with us cats looking like a hot, west coast garage band on a night out, we was in past the bouncers and sharkin' for peaches.

Meanwhile, back at my family homestead, Ma handed me a brown paper bag with some food for the trip and we all embraced and cried and laughed and waved as I hopped in beside Sly, and he drove us off, heading out of the city.

So, there I was, end of June 1974, first day of summer recess on the cusp of a fine adventure. I was 16 years old, light brown sun-streaked hair covering my ears, flared jeans covering my Converse sneakers, with *MC5* and *Grateful Dead* patches covering my denim jacket lapels.

The first day of my summer vacation, preparing for my western odyssey from New York City to Wyoming; which might as well have been Mars for all I knew about the place. Wasn't that where cowboys lived, and rattlesnakes? Hell, this could be dangerous. I knew my way around the city streets but the wide open was kinda big and wild, and open.

Also In my bag was the thing dearest to me at that time; a big battered old book about American Folk music; of the Blues men and women of the south, Roots and Country from the Appalachians, Cajun style from New Orleans, and creole, spiritual and gospel descended from the slave days. But I was a living listening sponge for all kinds of music. If it grooved then I was *"gone man, solid gone"* as Baloo once said in *'the Jungle Book'*.

But the purpose of my trip was to not only read about my passion, but to learn how to feel it too. To imbibe, soak up and become as one with the sounds.

Sly was headed to Baltimore, and as a favour to mom, he took me in his 1958 Cherry Red Chevrolet to catch the bus from there.

Chapter 10

Go West

We left New York and hit the Interstate and Sly told me all about his latest doings. He'd gotten married just two days before and was in high spirits, though the band thing wasn't going so well. They was just hangin' round waiting for him to get his act together, which he wasn't. Except he did write *'Family Affair'*, and played most of the instruments on it, too. So, he wasn't as crazy as people made out. He was alright by me, though and I loved the guy like the brother I never had.

Sly taught me all about laying a rhythm, then picking out a melody on his guitar, laid across his lap as he drove south to Maryland on that hot summer's day in '74. Folk had a more cavalier approach to road safety back then.

'It's not the teaching, it's the learning.' He said. And I learned to watch the road and hold on to the wheel while that cat picked away at the strings and sang little lines.

We talked about fashion and style and music and life, and love. It was strange, but I kinda felt like we *were* kin. There was a connection, a brotherly bond. Something primal and real.

It was an enlightening experience and I was thirsting for knowledge. And Sly kept pouring the bottle of realization 'til I was intoxicated with colour and vigour and zest, and a little ouzo too, which he kept in the glove box.

We parted company at Baltimore, Sly later flying west to Santa Monica, and me giggling and singing *'It's a family affair, hic.'*

'Hang loose Randy, my man.' Sly advised me, as he grinned his big toothy smile. Then he was gone and I turned to head into the depot, waiting on the Greyhound for my Western adventure to the land o' the buffalo.

I took a seat upfront near the driver. Now here's a top tip for y'all. If you choose the front seats, you mostly get the double seat to yourself. People will get on the bus and always assume there's a whole double seat back there, somewhere and will pass you by. And as we all know, when you assume, you make an *ass* out of *u, me* and *everybody*. Course, half way along the aisle, when the realization hits them that there ain't a double seat left, they cain't turn back. That's when they got to play the 'fellow passenger' game. Who's looking the least offensive to sit next to? And who looks like they may get off soon, or snores, or has ferocious bodily odours, or is spreading out to intimidate, or has a gun stuck in their waistband or any number of things.

Well I had my double seat up top with a clear view of the road ahead, and Glen Campbell on the radio, and no smelly dude sweating and panting next to me. Another trick is to rummage in your bag on the seat next to you, as someone gets on. Avoid the eye contact, unless it's some pretty young thing.

We took off and set forth into the great unknown via Pittsburgh, Indianapolis, St. Louis, Kansas, and across the Great Plains. It was a long journey and I arrived in Denver, late Friday night where the bus terminated.

I found a little motel/guest house dive across the street, and dumped my bag. But I was too excited to sleep and headed out into the cool Colorado night air.

Across the street, I came across a Jazz Bar called *Club Baja*, a smoky urban kind of joint and followed a party of chicks straight in, my longish hair foolin' the guys on the door. One of Sly's old paisley yellow and red kaftans did the trick as well, but it wasn't exactly Jazz club attire.

I was in my first Jazz joint and felt right at home. This is where I belonged, with chicks and music and dancin' and colored lights, and colored chicks and white dancin' chicks. Remember I was sixteen and my blood was pumpin'.

Travel weary, but light on my feet, I hit the dance floor as the band thrashed away, creating a groove like nothing I'd ever heard.

A loud hi-hat was tapping out a rhythm, while a keyboard guy weaved a melody around it that seemed to sashay like a seductive stripper's strutting booty. Then a big dirty bassline joined in like a prowling hungry alley cat looking for a scrap. A tall, lean black guy in a small hat with sweat pouring down his brow punctured this beat with his bluesy horn, with swagger and swing. And these overlapping layers of sound affected me like a gospel revival and I was a mess of arms and legs, stompin' and slidin' on the dancefloor. I wasn't alone. The whole club seemed to be shaking to the beat. Oh, man, what a ride.

I was hypnotised by the lanky trumpeting hat dude. He had bulging eyes and inflating cheeks that all seemed to move independently of each other. I found out later that he was none other than Curly Bones Smitty, a delta bluesman who could twist his wiry frame all over the place when the beat took him. And with his left eye popping out and his right cheek near to exploding, he was a strange freak to behold. But damn, could he blow his horn. Then he'd switch eyes and his left cheek would blow up like a balloon. What a Jazz cat.

The singer called out between songs to keep the audience on the good foot, and the music pounded up an infectious primeval beat of Soul, Blues, Jazz and Country and everywhere I looked people were lost in their own scene, digging the beat and shuffling their feet.

At 3 a.m. I seemed to shake out of the joint and across the street into my lodgings. I had the craziest of dreams. Of shimmering lights and soft white skin and swirling hair.

'Randy, wake up! You'll miss your bus.' Said a bleary-eyed, but divine young lady as she shook me awake in the morning, her hair all tousled and half covering her pert yogi bear's noses. [Author's note- a colloquialism for breasts]

I don't know who she was, or where she came from, but she'd stuffed a muffin into my satchel, and I was up and out of my bed, pulling on clothes as I went, some of which were mine.

Next stop, Injun country as I caught the bus out of Colorado and then on and on through the Black Hills. I had to pull my jacket collar closer and adjust my newly acquired fishnet stockings under my jeans, as we climbed this way and that around jagged hills with sheer rock faces one side, and bottomless drops the other.

It felt like I was on a stage coach haring round the bend like something outta the wild west, being chased by whooping Cherokees. Hey, but this most definitely was the wild west. And I was in it, headed towards a meeting round the old totem pole myself. Crazy times.

At last. What a fine song that is, *Etta James, 'At Last'*. That song just takes me away. At last, the bus pulled into Cheyenne where I was to meet a distant relation from my mother's side, Uncle Ric. Or as he was known locally, *Flaming Thunderclap*, full blooded Arapaho Indian and the head of his tribe.

His instructions from old Mother Feelgood was to teach me spirituality, Indian style! And he held her letter in his hand like a Death Warrant.

Chapter 11

Going Back to my Roots

As I stepped, wearily down from the bus I was greeted by an apparition from hell itself. The bus released its airbrakes and there stood a huge great statue of a man in faded denim shirt, leather and tin lanyard around his thick, dark neck, and a great hook nose hammered into his stony features. The whole horror show was topped off by the shiny dome of his utterly bald head.

Uncle Ric frowned deeply, as I assumed a pleasant smile and open warm countenance.

'Hm, so you are young Randolph, Rosemary's youngest, huh?' he drawled, and it sounded like shingle being poured through a car fender.

'Yes, sir', I replied, keenly. Always best to be polite to a 'Red' man.

'I can see from the rude expression of disgust in your eyes...' he said, seeing right through my poker face, (gotta work on that)

'...that you were expecting me to have long hair, like in the movies.'

His coal-black eyes bored into the back of my head through my innocent wide eyes. Then he spat a phlegmy gob bullet square between my heels with such venom and speed, I plum froze. When I looked up again he was yanging his jaw, trying to get his teeth back in place.

'Well son, you long-hair, city livin', ornery, loathsome piece of offal, when a member of my family passes, I cut two inches from my braids.' He stared some more and to break the silence I looked once again at his glistening coppery bonce. This guy had seen a lot of tragedy, and left me feeling he may start on my hair next, or worse, my jeans.

'Hey, that's cool man,' I said. I was a little put out by his attitude by now.

He grunted by way of ending our little mutual greeting and I was directed to hop in the back of his Dodge pick-up truck for the journey back to his village.

Why I couldn't ride in the front became clear at our next stop, a farm on the outskirts of Cheyenne, as we pulled up and another Indian dude emerged from a road side stall to grab a cage of chickens from the front seat, feathers and dust flying all over.

Uncle Ric invited me to join him up front with a grunt, which I graciously declined; not wishing to soil my jeans with chicken dung, and on we drove.

We turned onto a dry, dirt track for the Reservation and after about an hour of being thrown about in the back of the truck, we'd arrived at our destination; a collection of wooden and stone shacks scattered amongst some trees and with a pretty little stream meandering through the village and on through the valley towards some far off hazy hills.

'Welcome to Indian country, son', said Ric as I tumbled from the tailgate. He'd softened somewhat, I could see and I guess we'd patched up our differences.

Throughout that hot and dusty day, I was introduced to the rest of the tribe, including Ric's cousin Chance Shakespeare and Chance's three-year-old daughter, Feather Shakespeare. She was a happy little tot, and, coincidently, we shared the same birthday. Spooky.

There was a movement among the Native Americans at that time to adopt English sounding names, and you don't get more English sounding than *'Shakespeare'*.

Sometimes this went awry. My uncle Ric, Chief Flaming Thunderclap went by Richard Oldham Smith, all very English, but his brother, Moonglow chose the handle *'Reverend Calico Joe Heathrow'*. Well, I guess it ticked a lot of boxes, and he was the Witchdoctor so who was I to argue with the dude. Don't mess wi' no man's religion. That's what I always say, even if he is rattling a tin can of small bones.

Every day, me and the Big Chief, Flaming Thunderclap Ric, drove out towards the hills, where the air was dry, fresh and still. Twisted and stunted dead trees took root amongst the rocks and the sand, skewering out of the ground like the wind-blown bones of some ancient satanic beast, blackened and brittle and bent.

We rounded the huge boulders in the Dodge then halted in a cloud of dry dust, as we pulled up. Then we climbed out and made day camp in the lee of some giant rock face.

We did this every morning and smoked a little Peyote, a psychedelic, hallucinogenic herb, made from some cactus. The Chief went into trances and summoned the spirits, with his wailing and howling. I shied stones at a tin can in the dusty sand, mercifully devoid of any bones.

He reached his hands to the skies as he spoke in his strange tongue, entreating the souls of his ancestors, which were also mine, I reckon. Then we drank a little from his bottle, passed the peace pipe and spoke about life and love and soul. It was a spiritual journey and my mind was expanding like my lungs as I inhaled.

As the sun became lower in the sky and turned blood red, we headed out to another village where I was guest of honour at a traditional Indian sweat lodge ceremony. Every adult male stripped naked and entered a straw covered hole in the ground heated by stones, with the ladies of the village pouring hot oil through the straw and over the heaving, writhing, oily copper bodies. I got a few laughs the first time, as I peeled my duds off. I'd forgotten I still had on the stockings.

I wriggled to the top of the greasy pile, gasping and sucking for air inside the fetid stench of humanity.

Moonglow Heathrow, the bone shaker was there, awakening the spirits and generally controlling proceedings and divi-ing up the smoke. He kept his baggy boulder holders on as he thrust away chanting 'way o way, way o way, way o way', as Injuns are inclined to do, and slapping me in the chops with his unbound mystical snake, a-writhing around inside his loose-fitting jocks. Most disconcerting but hell, it was a sausage fest, and what goes on in a tepee stays there. I know I came out with a battered eye.

It all sounds barbaric, but afterwards, I felt refreshed and cleansed of all my inhibitions (not that I had many, y' understand) and eagerly drank from the gourd as it was passed around. By this time, we was sat round a crackling fire out on the plain next to the village. This gourd was kind of like a ceremonial drinking pot and contained a noxious smelling brew which tasted like a sweet flat beer. Not unpleasant if you held your nose and closed your eyes to stop them stinging. But it was the strangest thing. I felt euphoric and cleansed of all negative thoughts. Didn't have none anyways, but that was the best damn medicine I ever had. And I'm talking about being focussed and alive. Reduced the swelling from my black eye, too.

Then there was a torch-lit feast with Buffalo meat, sweet potatoes and corn all washed down with Mescal, a mind-bending liquor made from cactus juice and a secret Indian ingredient that I didn't enquire too heartily about, having heard occasional screams from the locals throughout the night.

It was a happy shindig with dancing and cavorting and Indians slapping themselves with drunken laughter. I stayed in my seat, my jaw aching from the smile of joy on my drunken face. Some guys were banging on some skin-covered drums, and there was a guitar, banjo and washboard in the mix too. I swear I heard a fiddle and I guess cowboy music had been accepted. Too soon if you ask me, with all that rivalry you see in the movies.

What with the moon-juice and the banjo twanging, I learned to 'feel' rather than see or hear the music, and I seemed to float around the table and I knew I was dancing and being slightly hypnotised by a bright pair of dark brown eyes, as I swirled around in a heady fug of liquor and herb and musky scent.

Next morning, I awoke in my room naked except for an eagle feather, plaited amongst my adolescent curls, nestled amongst my little fella. And I felt light and bright and bouncy as I dressed and strutted over to Ric's pad for our daily trip to the desert. Village life continued with some old guys loafing around in the shade and kids joshing and kicking a ball. Mamas were gossiping and laughing in their sing-song voices and the menfolk were going about their business.

Business seemed to be making stuff for the tourists. Bracelets, beads, dream catchers and moccasins were all sewn, made, chewed, stitched and boxed up. Pick-ups came and went bringing materials in and taking boxes of this and that out for retail. Tourists just couldn't get enough of all that old tat as they poked around Denver, Boulder and the Yellowstone Park and old battle fields.

I got used to the village life and strutted around in my multi-coloured duds. The strange stares I'd got at the beginning soon disappeared and I actually started to enjoy the company of these people. They were dirt poor, y' understand. But much the same as you and me, with dreams, desires and aspirations, and a cavalier attitude to personal grooming. (This being unlike me).

Over the years, I've donated a lot of my old clothes to some of the little dudes there. It dang near breaks your heart seeing these kids running around dressed in rags, with no proper education, not enough food to eat if the crops failed, and pooping in a trench in the woods.

But what really broke my heart was the truly pitiful sight of them wearing my hand-me-down cravats around their heads as they whooped around, being Indians. Even though they was.

On my last day at the village we drove out to the desert as usual. But this time I must have fallen asleep, during our usual schedule. I had nightmares of sounds, and rhythms and sweaty cannibals dancing round flames as great vats of bubbling liquid steamed over fires.

I awoke, gasping for air, cradling an empty bottle of Mescal, all alone and ravaged with thirst. I had no concept of how long I'd been there and was just contemplating drinking my own brew, if you catch my drift, when *'a girl, my Lord in a flatbed Ford, such a fine sight to see'*, rolled up and invited me to jump in. What a beauty.

Well, the sun was beating down and it was almost like I was Robinson Crusoe stranded on a desert island, when suddenly a boat sails into the harbour, metaphorically speaking. I had no notion of how many days I'd been left in the desert and could only nod a greeting as I gingerly climbed up into the front passenger seat. My lips were chapped and my throat felt like sandpaper as I tried to swallow to speak.

Chapter 12

Heaven Must Be Missing An Angel

This heavenly angel, for that's how she appeared to me, handed me a flask of water and it trickled over my cracked lips and down my parched throat until gradually I felt able to ask who she was.

'Oh, I'm a friend of Mr. Thunderclap's. He asked me to come by 'n pick y'all up as he was called back to the village.'

'How long have I been out here?' I gasped.

'Couple of hours' she replied.

Well, that was a surprise, and as I let this piece of insight sink in, I took a sideways look at the lady sitting next to me as she drove along over the unpaved road, eyes fixed ahead, slim hands on the wheel.

There were masses of lustrous platinum blonde hair pulled up and back in a ponytail, beautiful piercing blue eyes and little bow lips, painted bright red. She had clear, pale skin and a slim neck, with a delicate little dimple between her collar bones just peeking out from the unbuttoned neck of her green chequered flannel shirt.

But as my eyes devoured her, I couldn't help but notice the most fulsome bust that my eyes had ever seen, except my Mama's. But these beauties weren't strapped in and held up by a pinafore. They defied any kind of confinement, or gravitational pull (also, unlike mama's) and strained against the fabric of her embroidered waistcoat.

What a rack! And them buttons were in danger of shooting off in all directions. As was I.

Double stitched perhaps.

My throat constricted and I took another slug of water while trying to avert my gaze and stop dribbling.

'I'm Dolly, by the way. You must be Randy.'

'Yes, I am, ma'am'. I managed to squeak. I gulped again, my cardboard tongue sticking to the roof of my mouth.

So, that was how I tagged along in fine company as I made my way east to begin my career in International Superstardom.

It was the start of another adventure at first, as we pulled in to the Reservation to say my goodbyes to my new Native American friends, and to little 'Tinkling Bell Deer woman', who I'd become well acquainted with in her little tepee, earning me the Indian handle "Man who creeps on bent knees makes ground shake."

Those pesky Indian fools had shortened it of course. Now I was plain old 'Randy Kneetrembler.' I was reminded of this for ever after by any visiting red cousin from then on in. It was a term of endearment to them, and well, it could ha' been worse, I guess. I got a cousin somewhere who goes by "Boy has big dinner, defecates behind hut", which shortened to 'Shitting bricks'. Like I said, could have been worse.

I couldn't wait to be on the road again. This was partly due to Tinkling Bell setting her cowboy hat in my direction, and getting hooked up was not on my agenda just then. I was a free spirit and intended to stay that way. We'd had some fun, learning biology. And I'd certainly used my new-found spirituality to 'feel', rather than see. Mostly 'cos it was pitch dark when I crept into her little shack. It was fun times foolin' around with my sweet little squaw giggling and fondling and dancin' around my totem pole.

I stopped by and thanked Uncle Ric for his hospitality and spiritual awakening. To be honest the stink from the village would've driven me off into the night anyhow, but for Dolly's appearance. So, it was handshakes and back slapping all round, and some slobbery kisses from the more fetching females. I shook hands and bowed respectfully to the less attractive ones, mostly cos they were all whiskered and prune-like.

Off we drove, in the hot, dry summer heat, east, out of Cheyenne, then on Interstates. All the time listening to Country and Western. Yeah, two types of music. Occasionally we'd mix it up a little by checking out some AOR shows, occasionally some black stations all the way into Tennessee and through great fields of cotton. Nashville was where Dolly was heading and I knew that was gonna be the end of the road for this little trip.

On the journey, we stopped just outside of Kansas City where there was this buzz going on. We passed mile upon mile of people walking, hippy vans tootling along and everyone heading to a place called Sedalia, Missouri, just north of the Ozark hills.

Suffice to say, that's where I got spellbound, bewitched and hoodwinked into thrumming on the bass guitar in front of an estimated audience of 100,000 people and got my rock on with some crazy cats for a long hot weekend. And along the way had a meeting with the Devil himself.

It was probably the biggest Rock festival you've never heard of. The Ozark festival, and I'll set down the stories in my Rock themed book one day, as it's sorta unrelated to my current tale.

We left early morning, three days later, after it was all over and continued our road trip. On the way, we'd gotten real close and it was the most intense kind of experience a young man could have with an older chick. She was twenty-four, going on eighteen, with a bright and bubbly innocence, but a drive and ambition to succeed. Which she did, of course.

There was a real hollow feeling on our last night together in a Motel in Clarksville. Dolly put on her sunglasses and cowboy hat – her standard disguise, and off we went to eat. That girl had an enormous appetite.

'My weaknesses have always been food and men – in that order', she said to me, more than once. I took no offence. Heck, I knew I was just passing through, and glad to make her acquaintance. But also, I think, I just plain ol' fell in love with her on the miles of road behind and ahead of us that summer.

She had a way with words and also opined,

'A peacock who rests on its feather is just another turkey.' This was in the restaurant and by now, of course, the waiter was getting impatient, I could see.

'Look Lady, like I told ya, we got the steak, we got the ribs, we got shrimp, we got chicken, plenty of chicken. We don't got no fancy pantsy boids of paradise. Now, can I get you something to drink, or are you ready to oider? Sheez!'

Not a Midwesterner, I was guessing.

We celebrated that last night together at the Red Lobster Bar & Grill in downtown Clarksville with a banquet. There were indeed ribs, chicken, steak with fries. Everything the insolent waiter had recommended, in fact and beetroot salad all washed down with wine and beer. A Nashville band played in the corner with a guy called Jimmy Buffett on vocals and guitar which struck me as a strange sounding name, like he was a diner or something.

Many years later I reminded him of that place when we was yackin' 'bout songs and melodies and record companies and stuff.

'There's something missing in the music industry today, Randy, and its music. Songs you hear don't last, it's just product fed to you by the industry,' he told me.

Well, that's as maybe my friend but at the time you was swinging your Stetson around in my Club, a-hooting and a-hollering, sucking on a long curly straw at a Margeurita, with someone else's vomit dribbling down the front of your Plaid shirt, as you line-danced to the *Village People's 'YMCA'*!

Yep, *It's '5 o'clock somewhere'* all right. I never have a Marguerita yet, without thinking of my pal Jimmy and his songs that seemed to float your little sailboat away to a palm tree island, someplace. Luckily, I managed to gloss over the dribbling vomit recollection.

A friend of Dolly's joined us for dinner that night, name of Polly or Molly and they could have been twin sisters. Like two peas bursting outta the same pod with their masses of blond curls, thrusting bosoms and two rows of perfect white teeth when they laughed, which they did, often. Come to think on it, she may have been Holly. A spikey little doll with hot red berry lips.

After dessert, we left the restaurant and took a stroll back to the Motel. The crickets were chirruping and a light breeze carried the scent of jasmine and mud to mingle with the musk from the bouncing blonde curls of Dolly and Polly/Molly.

Dolly started getting all soppy and maudlin and began to half hum and half sing to me, all dewy eyed. It was a song she'd been toying with the whole day and we was making up verses and adding words. She called it *'I Will Always Love You'*, and was a big song for her at the time, though it was new to me. It sounded 10th grade school-girly bubble-gum Pop at the time, and we laughed as we changed some of the lyrics and took out the bit where she sang 'Randy made me feel good' and I was mightily flattered and didn't I tell her so!

It went on, of course to be one of the biggest selling hits of the Century, when Whitney Houston butchered it with her wobbly lip rendition. But I preferred Dolly's version, even with my added lyrics, and luckily, I was kept off the writing credits for contractual and matrimonial purposes.

Polly/Molly went on ahead by this time, to get to bed early. She was driving the rest of the way, in order for Dolly to be nice and rested for some shows in Nashville.

We got back to the motel room a little drunk and giggly while I excused myself to make a call home. I'd recently celebrated my seventeenth birthday and knew Mama Feelgood and my sisters would be missing me, as I was missing them.

Call over, I headed back to the room and knocked gently on the door before letting myself in. The lights were off and I could just see by the faint bluish glow of the street light in the parking lot, as it filtered through the thin cream curtain, and fell on to the wonderful bountiful curves of my dream girl.

I'd had many a teenage fumbling up until this point in my youth. But that was the night that this boy became a man and I slipped the sheet slowly and tightly over her curves and wallowed in the wonderful yearning embrace of that beautiful and demanding and sensual woman.

I slithered in beside her hot body. We were like two snakes entwined. Eager yearning bodies wanting to touch in every place as the fan above moved the warm air around our hot lovemaking. As soon as I put my lips on her stomach, she arched her back and reached for me with searching hands to guide me to a warm place. Well every place was warm and our sweat-slicked bodies just slipped around in our horny grappling.

Afterwards, I was a wreck. Physically drained and gasping at the thick, stifling air.

Later on, I slipped out and went back to Dolly's room and snuck under the covers on toes of twinkle. I'd made a good friend in Dolly, but I knew she was semi-married and that action kinda played on my conscience. I like to at least have the opportunity to accept an invitation or permission first.

However, as Polly/Molly once said, 'there'll always be a little bitty Randy in me.' Right on sugar dumplings. Plus, she wasn't married, I think. Good times.

It was a *'ships passing in the night'* situation, though she'll always have a special place in my heart, along with all the rest of the chicks I've fallen in love with over the years.

But I did bump into Dolly, again, literally. It was at her birthday bash which I helped to organise at Studio 54. We embraced as friends do, and gassed away like we'd parted only yesterday. She knew all along I'd had a lustful eye on Polly/Molly or Holly and I got the feeling that she had found it funny, and even set Polly/Molly up for me, in a strange pimp-like way.

She was a big star now, of course and got quite uppity, but in a nice, teeth-dazzlingly smiley way when some record company guy took her arm to meet some other faceless sap.

We managed to sneak a snuggle before the night was out, and it rekindled a dormant flame within me.

'Hey Randy, this bird has flown, dude,' I reminded myself and headed back to my delightful companion for the evening, Linda Lovelace who was giving me tips on eating fruit, I remember.

Now, here's a sliding doors/parallel universe thing, we got right here. Cos I found out years later that Dolly and Holly (Polly/Molly?) may have been look-a-like tribute singers. Yeh, how d'ya like that caper? Ol' Randy hoodwinked by a coupla saucy females. And one of 'em was Candy Pikestaff, the country-blues singer.

America is a whole heap o' land and Dolly Parton was a rising star in '74. Entrepreneurs would put 'Dolly' on the road to capitalise. And lots of busty blond singers were recruited to play all over the place. In fact, there was a Dolly Parton look-a-like competition in Tennessee one time and the real Dolly Parton came 4th! Incidentally, I came in 5th. She was big business and there was a lot of recruiting. I had to sadly decline an offer to gig in Canada, but my Dolly, and Polly were busy singing and playing towns all over, even Nashville.

This was a scene dreamt up way back in the 'sixties by Motown execs. The Temps, Four Tops, Supremes, etc. was huge acts and television was relatively new. No-one could see their faces that clearly. At one point, there was seven *Four Tops* groups on tour round the States at the same time. I know cos my three sisters were in one version, all moustachio'd up with a shop window dummy as the fourth member. They was billed as *the Four Tops show* in case anyone complained. But they never did. And cos there was only three of 'em, well, the fee was split three ways. Kerching!

Radio Randy 1975

(ARE YOU READY) DO THE BUS STOP – THE FATBACK BAND

FIGHT THE POWER – THE ISLEY BROTHERS

GET DOWN TONIGHT – KC AND THE SUNSHINE BAND

LOVE HANGOVER – DIANA ROSS

DECEMBER '63 (OH WHAT A NIGHT) – FRANKIE VALLI

K-JEE – MFSB

SOUL CITY WALKIN' – ARCHIE BELL AND THE DRELLS

WHY DID YOU DO IT – STRETCH

PASTIME PARADISE – STEVIE WONDER

DON'T TAKE AWAY THE MUSIC – TAVARES

A mixed bag here as Disco tries to dominate, with pop and pure funk still keepin' on keepin' on, and Stevie off on a Latin trip, with a funky drip.

I've included K-Jee here, not only cos it's a great song, but also it was a track that came out of the sound of Philadelphia, or TSOP. And also here, we have MFSB. TMA if ya asking me. (That's 'Too Many Acronyms'). Some say that MFSB stood for Mother Father Sister Brother. Or was it Mother Heckin' Son of a Gun?

It's a little-known fact that it actually means *Mozart Feelgood, Soul Brother* (Mozart being my given middle name, after my great great, great granddaddy, Wolfgang Amadeus).

I'd been swinging one night in the Catfish and these Soul cats came in looking all pimped up in shades and long fur coats. Stood out somewhat as it was August and a hundred degrees and the air was hot and sticky in the joint as the crowd grooved to my mojo.

They were Philly boys identifying the New York sound and putting a more industrial style to it. I'm positive they pinched some of my ideas. But mimicry is the greatest form of flattery, so they say. So is flattery.

'Love Hangover' just starts all summery and kicking back in the grass and lazin' on a sunny afternoon 'til, woah! Hold on baby, I'm coming. Got to be my absolute favourite Diana Ross song and she was all lined up to follow it up with that old Teddy Pendegrass song, 'Don't leave me this way', when Thelma Houston's take on it started pulsing through the speakers of every Disco in every City. I convinced Motown to release it as a single, despite my deepest regard for Miss Ross.

But I just can't seem to squeeze Thelma in. My dance card is too full, if you catch my drift, and that is a crying shame. For Thelma. Maybe I'll make her my number eleven substitute. And give her a rub down in case I need to bring her on.

Chapter 13

Yum Yum, Gimmee Some

When you're up there, in the spotlight on stage or in your little DJ box, you gotta understand people are looking at you. Well they certainly was looking at *me*, hot jiminy. You are the performer, and you better perform or they'll go someplace else, like the Bingo, or a Juice bar, or the gas station. You gotta look good, and hopefully I can give you a few tips along the way.

'Hair is the first thing, Randy. And teeth the second. Hair and teeth. A man got those two things he's got it all.' That's what Mr. James Brown told me as we shared a double glass of Babycham and Cherry Tizer at the Electric Lady Garden Bar on 5th Avenue.

Everyone was hanging out at the Lady Garden in the '70's 'til it was closed down due to technical difficulties and personal hygiene issues.

We was having one of our irregular *"Functioning Music-aholics Anonymous"* meetings, with the emphasis on Funk. I usually hosted 'cos the Lady Garden was where it was happening at the time. Plus, it was my crib.

On this particular occasion, the discussion had turned, neatly from shirt cuffs to male grooming. We were hashing together a sort of men's guide to beauty, and were getting down to some serious gum-flapping.

'Damn right, Mr. Brown', I replied. 'That's what I am talking about JB, Minister of New Super Heavy Funk'. He really did call himself that, by the way, on his 1975 tour. What a guy.

'And, the one thing that can solve most of people's problems is dancing.' He opined, scattering yet another off-piste statement to change the subject.

'Now hold on Godfather of all things funky, we is talking hair, teeth and facial care, here. Don't be all complicating matters, like *ZZ Top* trying to play *"Papa's got a brand-new bag"* here.'

'No, Randy. I mean your hair and teeth, they gotta be tight. But loose'.

'Fine, fine, foxy lady, baby get on down, yeah. Tight but loose, like *Led Zeppelin*.' And I sang it more than I said it.

'Say what?', said JB.

'Tight but loose, James. In control but bending the rules. Like a fist of steel in a velvet glove. Dancing close with a beautiful woman with the radio playing your favourite song. The power of individuality.'

'Three Wheels on My Wagon', he said

'That's what I'm saying, James. Er, what the, what you say?'

'By the *New Christy Minstrels*. That's my favourite song 'n I ain't gonna mess around while *that* record is on no radio.

'What you talkin' 'bout Willis.' I said. His outburst had brought back the image of my dear uncle Thunderclap and his horror mask of a face and whooping Indians. 'Tight but loose, James. Tight but loose.' I was attempting to get the chit chat back on track and on the good foot. But he was off on a nostalgic tangent I could tell, and singing in pure abandon.

'Those Cherokees are after me...' he went. Then his eyes lit up, he inhaled deeply, his full-lipped mouth seeming to tremble. There was a silent pause. Then he let out one of his screams.

'Yeeeeooooowwwwwwwwwwlll'

It gave me such a fright I fell backwards right onto Bootsy Collins' Bass guitar standing next to the settee. In my attempt to steady myself and protect such a fine-looking instrument of Funk, and his guitar, I accidently picked out two Funkasaurus power bashing Bass notes, in the key of F (F for Funk naturally). And dang me if Bootsy didn't retrieve his axe and start plucking away at the thing, picking out the same notes in tandem sequence, while young Nile Rodgers joined in the jam and chopped away on his guitar, right on cue.

By this time the hook was in me and the devil's ear-potion had entered my brain, once again. I power-hopped off the sofa and was cavorting with JB's personal travelling candelabra.

'Get Up Offa That Thing.' He called out, all possessive-like, and this time we was all getting' down just for the funk of it. Inadvertently we had created the intro to one of James Brown's monster hits and I tapped out a double fast eight beat on a tin platter with my jewelled rings, just to add some trills.

Up until then, it had been a quiet night at the Garden. Noon on a Tuesday as I recall and I was just grateful that Maceo Parker wasn't there too, blowing his saxophone horn and shattering my relaxation time, and my glasses!

Bootsy was playing with *Funkadelic* at the time, but he and Mr. Brown used to hang out and we'd all talk jive and try and create or discover the fabled and mystical missing Funk chord, during that hazy lazy spring of '76.

I remember James Brown and Quincy Jones were trying to explain the theories of music to my keen mind.

Now, music is kind of in my blood. It's also my middle name. Well, Mozart is, like I said. And the theory went something along the lines of three notes played together was a chord.

bout two notes, Quince?' I asked. He shook his head,
er who's heard many questions like this. But from
n kids.

a chord, Randy'.

'I believe, you'll find that it's actually two notes played together'. I replied, triumphantly and reached for my tumbler of the sparkling stuff. Conversation over, and one point to Randy.

'Humph', growled Quincy and went back to his philosophy book.

Interesting character, Quincy Jones. Worked with Billie Holliday, Louie Armstrong, Dizzy Gillespie, Miles Davis, Aretha Franklin, Michael Jackson, Frank Sinatra, Tony Bennett, rappers and all sorts. And me. Probably the only one who can say *that*.

After a few cocktails and some agitated pencil chewing, the spirit within me rose and there seemed to have occurred a kind of epiphany.

'I got it! Yeah baby, Randy's got it.' I said.

'G flat minor 7th over D sharp with an added 5th. With an F sharp 9.' I blurted out while it was fresh in my mind.

'Randy, you dang fool', cried Bootsy. 'Add on a sus 4, or a diminished sus 4 and you got something.' Then he fell asleep.

As did we all. The Garden had luxurious sofas and it was a drowsy kind of afternoon spent napping in the sumptuous embrace of soft, artificial fur-upholstered settees. 'Til my lady, Melody woke us all up with a platter of hot buffalo wings, cucumber, celery, carrots and dips. But not before she'd woken me up with a downstairs fondle. Just to get my blood moving, the brazen she-devil.

Of course, by then the missing chord, once discovered, was now lost again as we'd all forgotten it in a heady fug of champagne and smoke. And I can't exactly be sure I got all the letters and all the numbers right. I'll have to call up my friend Bruno Mars. That cat 'll know for sure.

At least we managed to get the hair and teeth thing down on my note pad, or else that would've been lost, too.

Anyways, so my carefully blow dried and Brylcreemed chicken-winged hair took on more of a coiffured bouffant, and my hairdo became a bit more refined from its earlier formative days. It's vital to look good and I highly suggest adding on a little face furniture with the addition of sideburns. An inch below the ears, no more, and a moustache curving around the upper lip and tapered to a point, a half inch below the mouth line, and you're one smokin' Adonis.

Hair styles changed throughout the 'Seventies, but not a great deal for men. Sometimes I 'tached up, sometimes not. We like the classic look. Hippies and Punks had varying ideas on the theme, too.

The classic cut for ladies of the time was the Farrah Fawcett look. With the flick either side of a centre parting. By the late 'Seventies, it all ended up in a disastrous hairstyle faux pas, with the perm. That hairstyle was fine with my black brothers and sisters, but just looked like all the honkies was permanently startled in'78. Marc Bolan wore it well, however. But that was more of a corkscrewy affair. *And* he was a cool cat.

It's important to be healthy too, as you're in the spotlight, brother, literally! Eat well, lots of meat, fruit and vegetables. I'm never too far away from a pineapple, it's good for the skin. Eat raspberries and it's good for your *lover's* skin. Mm hmm, finger lickin' good.

My Sunday ritual was always the same from childhood. We was influenced, food-wise, by my flaky dad as kids growing up. A traditional family British roast dinner, with beef or lamb, potatoes, carrots, parsnips, peas, carrots and thick gravy. Mama was the best cook I ever knew and us kids never went hungry. Then the next day you can skim off the lardy cooking fat and meat juices out of the roasting tray. And spread all that fatty, scummy goodness on your toast for added vitamins. Oh man, I'm just full of protein and hot cookery tips.

You got to be fit, too. All that movin' and a-groovin' can tire you out, man. I watch a lot of basketball on the TV and that's good for the heart, keeping them blood lines open. Jogging became the thing too, in the '70s. But I don't relate to all that huffing and puffing. My rule is, don't run if you ain't being chased.

Now dancing will keep you in shape. After I turned sixteen, my big sister, Loretta would sneak me into the *Shakin' Hand* on East 115th Avenue in Harlem, where she worked. The kids want a little action, and there I could cool down and burn off a little steam, hitting the floor and doing the *'Locomotion'*.

It was a Soul food bar, serving burgers and fries with a hot 'n sweaty dance floor through an archway, a bar at one end.

One night the owner spots me and grabs a hold of me, angry that some kid had gate crashed his joint. Ike was the big man on the scene just then. He owned a handful of dives and tonks and was the go-to guy for lots of movie producers back then. The big movement of the early 'Seventies was the Blaxploitation genre. Ike knew someone and ended up as consultant and dialect coach on a few movies. Liked to think of himself as John Shaft. And no one understood him like his woman, Mrs. Shaft. She was the real boss, of course.

'What you doing here, you freaky deaky white punk boy.'

'Wassup Shaft.'

And that was when Loretta spotted the ruckus and high-tailed it out from behind the counter, scared for me and also for her job. And thank Otis she did, 'cos Ike was winding up a haymaker, with his shirt sleeve all tight, and stretched across his biceps. My crew had scattered and I was doomed.

'It's Okay, Ikey, honey. He's my baby brother', she said breathlessly, waiting for Ike to explode.

'How'd you get in here boy?' He asked, hands on hips when he'd dragged me off the dancefloor and into the kitchen, where it was quieter.

'On dancin' legs through an open back door.' I said, and I looked him dead in the eye. It's a gift, being able to communicate on any level.

'Why you back-chatting son of a gun, goddam shootin' your mouth off...'

'Hey, cool it brother. Ain't causing no trouble, just dipping my hip and movin' to the groovin'. Got a lotta respect for ya, man, and this is the swingingest joint in town.' And I articulated on the theme. Stroking his ego and giving constructive advice and generally telling him his club was *'Superbad'*.

Well that kind of compliment will win a dude over in no time. Forget the fact that his brows had knitted together and his eyeballs were popping from his straining head. He just loved his club, like he loved the ladies, when Mrs. Shaft wasn't looking of course.

So, I was put to work in the kitchen. Well, I was stood there anyways, getting eyeballed by Ike Shaft and him puffin' and pantin' and Loretta stroking his arm and nuzzling. He calmed down with a 'harrumph, goddamn...' and Loretta winked at me and set me to work. I knew she'd cool Ike down later with her womanly ways.

So now I was the chief of washing pots, with an apron over my head and chicken grease on the soles of my shoes. Man, I just couldn't stop dancin', even if I'd wanted to, which I didn't. Feet don't fail me, now, as I slipped and dipped amongst the grease and leftover bones and garnish and ketchup.

Next few weeks, I was washing them glasses and pots and pans, my arms going all over the place, like an octopus putting on a vest that's too tight. And I was hearing all these different Soul tracks and some early forms of Disco too. But also, I could hear beats in my head, and I just had to tap out the rhythm with my washing up brushes. Sometimes tapping to the beat, and sometimes on the off-beat and singing away in the kitchen in my natural baritone with an occasional quiet falsetto.

I didn't know, but out front, cats could hear my extra little percussion arcs and syncopations and were digging this new improvised supplement to the song that was playing. It's what you might call a remix, nowadays. What I had actually discovered was the nucleus of the Disco beat, and I was in total ignorant bliss in my wigged out soapy euphoria.

Dancing 'll sure keep you primed and defined. Not an ounce of flab did I have cluttering up my perfect physique. I was a teen on the scene and just a-bursting with soul energy. Plus, it was hot in that kitchen. It was like a work-out every shift.

Radio Randy 1976

GET UP OFFA THAT THING – JAMES BROWN

I WISH – STEVIE WONDER

CAR WASH – ROSE ROYCE

LOVE REALLY HURTS – BILLY OCEAN

I BELIEVE IN MIRACLES – THE JACKSON SISTERS

YOUNG HEARTS RUN FREE – CANDI STATON

DADDY COOL – BONEY M

SHAKE, SHAKE, SHAKE – KC AND THE SUNSHINE BAND

PLAY THAT FUNKY MUSIC – WILD CHERRY

YOU SHOULD BE DANCIN' – THE BEE GEES

This is Disco. Funk is taking a little back seat here, and allowing the younger musical reincarnation to stretch the fabric, somewhat. But you can't keep James Brown down when he's got the funky flame burning bright. And check out the bass riff on Wild Cherry.

But it's all about the sequins and dancin', on these ground-breaking cuts that still stand up today.

'Live like you wanna live, baby. Ain't nobody gonna bother you.' As Chuck Berry once preached.

'You wanna get felt? Sure you do! Get felt at Bob's felt roofing store. Our team has the necessary qualifications to check your sheathing and shingle. Free flashing on jobs over $20. Get felt today at Bob's over on Franklin Avenue.'

Chapter 14

Oo-bop, toto-toto-toto-toto, fa,fa,fa,fa, Fashion

All the top fashion designers were hanging out in the Apple in the '70s. The place to be seen to be *in* the scene

Of course, I would hang out with them before and after my gigs, too. Sometimes during, as well. Strutting around the stage, doing my dancing and turns and suchlike. Heck, I was in high demand as a catwalk model. Hey, and I had the physique for it, too. The stage was my runway and many of the clothes designers of the time were clamouring and aching for me to show off their new get-ups. I was happy to oblige, which is one of my mottos.

I used to have a little rhyme about three of them being like a little pop band, you know, like *Emerson, Lake & Palmer*, or *Crosby, Stills & Nash*, or *Mary, Mungo and Midge*. I'd Rap over the microphone during the bridge and break in *'Apache'* by the *Incredible Bongo Band*. Perhaps the first ever Hip Hop song, maybe? It certainly is fine and funky and allowed me to stretch my chops and drop the bomb

'Hey, Halston, Gucci and Fiorucci.

Bri-nylon, polyester and brushed-felt, white sou'wester.

Your dicky bow is good to go,

But I need something a little more macho, ya know!'

Then I laid down some fat bass beat, something by James Brown, just to up the tempo, weaving in and out of the bongo beat. 'Course, that just tickled Nile and Bernard, who loved my little jive-phrasing and that jazz talking, and stuck that piece of nonsense in one of their songs, *'He's the Greatest Dancer'* by those saucy sassy sisters of soul, *Sister Sledge*. About me, so I'm told. And I believe it.

The '70's was a time when fashion designers were becoming celebrities in their own right. They were out on the town, going to showbiz parties, hangin' out at the fashionable clubs, like the Electric Lady Garden, the Marabou, 54, The Paradise, and all.

Giorgio St. Angelo, Yves Saint Laurent, Valentino. They were the beautiful people. They surrounded themselves with beautiful people, including me and it was good publicity, too.

Cravats are the thing, or any neck based attire. You can wear one in so many ways, but they have to be satin or silk. The skin around your neck can be delicate, and you don't want no damn rag chafing you all night; same with your underwear.

Point of fact, I was voted *'Cravat wearer of the Year'* four years in a row from 1975 – 1978, then lost out in '79 to David Soul, though I always call him 'Hutchy baby' on account of his rabbit-soft hair and his Starsky and Hutch character - Hutch.

'Hutchy baby, wassup. You is looking kinda shy 'n all.' I remarked to him one time at some awards thing in Hollywood.

'Oh, you know me, Randy. I'm an accidental actor. I prefer to sing, but people know me as Hutch', he responded, with a sigh.

'Go with it, partner.' I said, trying to reassure him.

'Oh, I know I must play the game. God blessed me with these Norwegian blue eyes and blond hair and I guess I'm handsome, but all my life I've tried to run away from my looks. It does make me feel a little uncomfortable.'

'Ever tried wearing a ski-mask?' I didn't say out loud.

I could tell he was over-analysing again, and was clearly feeling jealous at all the female attention I was receiving instead of him.

'You know what you need, Bunny.' I said.

'No. Thank you Randy, not another evening with your delightful friend, Sally.'

'No. Not that, Bunny hutch. You need to get yerself a cravat.'

'Huh, a cravat?' He was intrigued.

'Yeh, a cravat. It has style. It practically oozes culture. And best of all it distracts the eye from your beautiful face. That's why I wear one.'

He took my advice, as we know and never looked back. Though he still had his army of adoring fans. Next time we met up he hustled over to where I was standing, by the champagne waitress. I was discussing cocktails with bubbles as she tried to disengage my belt-buckle one handed.

'Thanks for the fashion advice Randy', says David, the waitress having strutted off to work the room. She'll be back, I thought.

'Hey, don't sweat it, Soul man. How's it going for ya?'

'I've got beautiful baby skin.' He remarked, all matter of fact like, and then he was dragged away by some TV Producer guy, the gorgeous hunk. David Soul, that is, not the ferrety, sweaty four eyes in the bow tie.

Well that very same week he's up on the stage, and dragging out a little scribbled acceptance speech from the back pocket of his Lee jeans. That was the thanks I got from recommending the Cravat; he goes and wins *MY* award! But you know a man's neck beauty is more important to me than putting another irrelevant tin pot in my purpose built mahogany cabinet with an empty space for 'Cravat wearer of the Year' Award 1979.

Lots of fashions and styles came and went during the 1970s and new ideas that seemed right on were sometimes just a passing fad. I remember one day feeling good to go as I rode the subway from my neighbourhood in Midtown Chelsea to meet my personal stylist, Princess Diana van Neuhausen at her *'appointment only'* boutique in Flushing Meadows.

I was travelling in my stretch denim sling-back two-piece chiffon-weave suit combination. Flared arms and trouser, but tight everywhere else. I was dressed to the left and travelling east and I was chafing all the way from the A zone to the E zone and all points Lower South side of the Bow Bridge.

When I got to Lady Di's I was wriggling about so much from the snugness of the cloth, I had to strip off and put on one of her wrap around gowns to ease the pressure.

Bianca was there also, as I recall, and it was a fun afternoon, as I hazily remember, trying on each other's clothes. And Diana, the wardrobe mistress, was throwing out ever more outlandish and garish blouses and garments for us to climb into and out of. I remember Bianca was hoping to purchase a slinky little number that she could wear whilst riding a white horse in Studio 54. Anything went back then, for sure. Whereas I just wanted something loose and unrestricting to ride the subway home.

There was a fashion at the time for reinventing oneself as European aristocracy and Diana had used that to great advantage with her cigarette holder and Jackie O glasses, but I knew her when she was plain ol' Betty Bonneville from Brooklyn. Occasionally she'd lapse into that nasal twang way of talking.

'Yeaaah Rianndy, honey, you wornna put orn that feather bowa wi' doze paints, shuga.' Saucy minx. And I wasn't actually wearing any pants at the time. Or anything else, for that matter. Except a smile. So, while Bianca was trying on dress number twenty-eight out back, Betty was playfully tickling me with a feather boa as she sat astride me, out front. I swear she had me bursting to be at her bouncer's, straining against my silk bound wrists. Hours later, the tension released, I slipped on a robe and crochet turban to ride home.

Another little outfit I had during my sparkly period during '77 was my gold lame lurex all in one cod piece and singlet leotard combo. One to be avoided at all costs, unless you happen to be performing some trapeze routines during a theatrical show of the *'Wizard of Oz'*. Again, chafing.

That was one ride on the subway I won't forget. I was getting stared at by the punks, who were a little put out that they was being *out-punked* man! By me! We got to talking, you know, cos Randy is hip to the people and I like to embrace new ideas and cultures. I wasn't *dans la monde* or *avec le vent*, as the French say, with the whole punk thing, but I did recognize one dude.

He was lookin' all surly with his lip all curled up like he was Elvis or trying to dry his teeth or somethin'. Black spiky hair and leather jacket. No shirt but a chain and padlock round his neck like he was catchin' the subway to go get his bike.

But you know, I kinda liked Sid. He was just a young punk lost in New York City and life; hanging with his homeys and heading to a club. He was a Bass-man like myself, so we had a connection right away and that was a fine club to be a member of. And despite the fact that Sid's fingers didn't look clean enough for no fat bass slappin', his girlfriend didn't seem to mind him playing hunt the marble up her sweater.

We got to talking and I remarked that he seemed to have a magnetism about him.

'I just cash in on the fact that I'm good looking, and I've got a nice figure and girls like me.' He said when he spotted me watching the frolicking. Well the last bit seemed true at least. Crazy Sid. Not at all vicious, just a lost boy in the big City, tweaking away on the subway.

We all ended up in CBGB's watching *Blondie* tearing the roof off the place. Drummer was a little off the beat, but who's looking at the sticks guy, when Debbie Harry is gliding around the stage.

Man, she was one sultry looking singer. Stood there on the stage giving sideways glances, high-heeled sneakers planted and tight sweater at attention. And what a voice. It soared over the clatter and banging that the band was making and softened it with her floating vocalizations.

They were a raw band, back then, learning their craft. But I could see they was going places. Even covered the old blues number *'Little Red Rooster'* with the main dude on slide. Sounded almost Country, Bluegrass, Bluesy.

During a break, she strode over and sat next to the punks, while I slid over in my gold hot pants making farty noises on the plastic seating.

'Who's your funny looking friend?' She asked.

'This here's Sid and Nancy.' I replied and reached out to caress a strand of sweaty hair from Debbie's glowing cheek.

Some other guy wandered over and took a shine to my ridiculous clobber, and we ended up trading clothes, and talkin' about two-minute Rock songs. He reminded me, a bit, of my younger self. He was tall and slim, with long hair and a fast draw, a gunslinger but no gun, just his ability to strike a pose.

I have to admit, I did feel a certain sense of conspicuousness as I curled on a pair of skin-tight jeans and his Ramones T-shirt. Joey

119

thought it a great scam and invited me on stage to do *'Blitzkrieg Bop'* with the boys, with me on maracas.

Then I went to Di's place, to try on her burlesque lingerie.

I always say to people 'be yourself', and I was always much more myself in a nice pair of flared slacks in something soft, like velveteen or moleskin; with silk or satin shirts, figure hugging. I sometimes wore a military jacket, or full length fur coat in winter with an out-sized baggy beret with a peak. Or a fedora. Oxford bags were another trouser that hung around for a while. Three buttons on the waist, naturally. Though I had five. With a snug man-made fibre waistcoat and bow tie. Hot shanks.

If you want to get a head, get a hat, and I can dig that. One of my hats gained worldwide fame when Prince wrote a song about my *'Raspberry Beret.'* A misunderstanding really. I'd just gotten a new tile and was wearing it at a party and Kim Basinger asked me for it.

'Randy, be a sweetheart and lend me your hat. It's freezing outside.' Kim was never one for the showbiz parties. It was just an opportunity for her to work the room and make connections, and look hot.

'Sure thing Kimmy, sugar dumplings. Here, have my old beret. Its sheepskin lined.' I always carried a spare hat, just in case.

And off she went, sporting my old red, suede number. I believe that's when she bumped into *'The Artist'* formerly known as *'Squiggle.'* Or Prince, as I called him. Lucky I wasn't packing my Pickelhelm, my customised German spiked helmet, or his song would have been a massive flop. Great for storing finger food and pineapple rings however, when you've got no pants pockets.

Come to think on it, *'Pickelhelm'* wouldha' scanned nicely instead of *'Purple Rain'*, another of Prince's smash hits.

'*Pickel-helm, Pickel-helm*'. Yeah, sounds spikey. Must give Mark Ronson a call. He's always begging me for ideas.

Of course, in any situation I always feel a little anxious if I'm without a cravat or neckerchief, craftily strung to one side allowing for a glimpse of my gold chain, nestled amongst my oiled chest hair.

When it comes to footwear, remember you're going to be in your shoes as much as you're in your bed, so make it comfy. Get yourself one of those 'Slumberease' King-sized numbers, not too hard, but definitely not too soft as it's bad for your spine. Get foam pillows instead of the feather variety as they are bad for the airways and you need to look after the voice.

My voice was my instrument and it spoke to people.

And go for something good for your feet too. Cuban heels were always a favourite, as well as Converse sneakers or bumper boots as I call 'em. Cowboy boots are also very comfortable and look mighty stylish in flares, whereas the good old standard moccasin is maximum comfort with minimum effort.

But, when I made guest appearances with the *Village People*, it was work jeans and steel-capped boots for my character, 'construction guy'. Me and David Hodo were great compadres as I already mentioned and we'd get up to some fine, high jinks, pretending to be each other.

He'd stand in for me at public appearances and red carpet events and shindigs, and I'd don his working gear for *Village People* gigs. Well, I had choreographed some of them dance routines, after all. It made a nice change to rough it occasionally, and at least I didn't have that enormous Red Indian headdress to worry about, neither. Them feathers, woah! Wheezy sneezy, sugar, and gave me the heebee geebees just thinking about that stinking sweat lodge out in the desert, and them damn chickens.

I was too young to go visit the troops in Vietnam during the early 'Seventies and I can't imagine the horror those guys had to go through. The only choice they had was to wear camouflage and combat military wear every day. Not cool. And it ain't kind to the skin, neither, being all rough, etcetera.

Not like silk or satin. But those fabrics do not take kindly to the heat and humidity of a South East Asian climate.

My advice to any comics or singers or bands is to check out the location of these war-torn conflict areas. And do some research before you go off and do your civic duty of cheering up the soldiers out there doing a fine job of keeping the world safe. Come see a professional for fashion advice. Give my secretary a call to make an appointment.

Radio Randy 1977

RUNAWAY – LOLEATTA HOLLOWAY

BEST OF MY LOVE – THE EMOTIONS

DANCE, DANCE, DANCE – CHIC

YOU AND I – RICK JAMES

MY FIRST MISTAKE – THE CHI-LITES

YOU MAKE ME FEEL – SYLVESTER

HAVEN'T STOPPED DANCING YET – GONZALEZ

DISCO INFERNO – THE TRAMMPS

EVERYBODY DANCE – CHIC

SHAME – EVELYN 'CHAMPAGNE' KING

Some powerful grooves blended perfectly with pure pop creating an electrifying four on the floor disco beat attack. Get in to the groove, it's makin' my body move. It's all getting hyper-flamboyant too, by now.

Sylvester was probably the first openly gay and outwardly black performer to come out and on to the scene, at this time.

Everyone knew that the gay community loved the Disco, but Sylvester let it all hang out. I even lent him some of ma's old blouses one night when he came around to my pad.

We was working on some song lyrics and he was flouncing around my sitting room, enjoying the freedom that only comes from wearing a large woman's dress, and humming this melody. I was doing a little vacuuming and singing, randomly.

'Do the hoovering up. In my towelling robe.'

Well, Sylvester just loved that jive and eventually he had a smash hit with *'Do You Wanna Funk.'* I claim no credit of course. Just happy to see the guy's big old chubby, rouged face with a jolly smile plastered on it. And to thank me, he came around every Tuesday to clean my apartment. His dustin' was truly shocking, but my pillows have never been so plumped up.

Chapter 15

Talkin' Loud And Sayin' Nothin'

You know what drives me crazy when I am out on the town, clubbing and discothequein'? Damn jocks. That's disc jockeys to you 'n me, not Scottish people, who I like by and large. With their red hair, tattoos on hairy muscly arms, and the ability to drink a gallon of beer without effecting their ability to articulate, unintelligibly. Same as when they was stone cold sober.

Ah, Brenda "Berwick Castle" MacKenzie. What a gal she was. She could drink me under the table that woman, then carry me home afterwards. And then dump me into my bed and have her wanton way with my prostrate form while I dreamed of babbling streams and summer days and naked dancers cavorting around a fire.

Then I'd open my bleary eyes and look up into the grunting face of a sweaty blotchy ginger gargoyle riding me like a Kentucky Derby winner. Didn't even get a rosette.

She was known as Berwick Castle Brenda 'cos she'd had whole armies of Scots and Irish and Englishmen take her defences from all gates, and crushed a few heads in her dark and smelly dungeon, too. You might say, a gal who knew what she wanted, and took it. Without asking. Even if she had asked, no one could have understood her. Or refused.

[Author's note – Berwick Castle, on the border between Scotland and England. A motte and bailey 12th Century castle that was invaded, and besieged numerous times by the English and Scots up until the 16th Century.]

So back to the tutorial, and those dang jocks, or DJs who take every opportunity to flap their gums (and I ain't talking 'bout

Brenda no more) before, during, and in the middle of every song they put on. Just can't help 'emselves. Goin' on and on, like a street bum wearing all of his clothes, 'bout nothin' in particular, and tryin' to sound cool. No, it is not cool. Your voice is an instrument, to be used wisely.

The microphone *amplifies* your voice. It's an amp just like pluggin' in your electric guitar or glockenspiel. You gotta know when to use your voice and for the right reasons. Example being, if you playin' some track, do not, and I repeat *DO NOT* crash the lyric. This is downright disrespectful to the artist.

Imagine you're in a club and you're swayin' away to the sumptuous melody of those British groovers *'The Real Thing'*.

'You to me are everything the sweetest...'

'Burger and fries, one ninety-nine',

'...oh baby, oh baby'

Well, that cat wants lockin' away in a cage and feeding with a catapult. Talk about killin' the mood with a food interlude. Not cool.

If you wanna say somethin', wait 'til the singer's finished his piece, then squeeze in your irrelevant sentence. Or you could give your message during the intro, but before the singer comes in, you dig? Or just shut the front door. Rap by all means, but there's a time and a place.

Very important also, is if yer gonna pipe up, the people need to hear what ya sayin'! They don't wanna be hearing nobody mumbling.

'Huronsphhnn. Hemmmonnhfff. Heh heh...'

'What! What he say, man?'

Set your levels right at the start of your night. Now me, for example, I have a Bass quality to mah voice so I just turn the dial back a little, set the top and the middle up a fraction. Yeah, there ya go. Check it out on a mic test with a 'ts, ts, ts' pushed out hard between tongue and teeth and make sure it's clear.

During the night, you may wanna adjust minutely. Remember to drop the fader on the track playin' slightly so you're not fightin' the record for speaker time.

Say it loud, but do not shout. Enunciate, articulate, and keep it short, wise guy. Who you talkin' to, huh? The guy at the front there, pestering you, once again to play *'I Love to Love'* by Tina Charles? No. You is talkin' to everyone in the room. So git your head up and let 'em see your eyes, and your hair. And talk proper English, like moi.

I always favoured the *Sennheiser* microphone, myself. But steered clear of actual proper headphones. They played havoc with my blue rinse demi-wave and I couldn't hear a damn thing, 'cept what was playing and what was lined up next.

I needed to hear what the *audience* was hearing. So I got Bobby D to rig me up the receiver piece of an old pay phone, and plugged that sucker in. I could clamp it to my ear and still listen to the monitor turned into the booth. I could also eavesdrop in on personal and intimate conversations happening around me.

Cute.

I always encourage people to come talk to me when I'm doing mah thang.

'Hi, what's your name, baby. That's cool. You got a number? Well, that's enough about you. Let's talk about me.'

Keep your fans happy. That's my motto. Another one, that is. And sometimes, some chick will ask for a song, you know and surprise you. Maybe a song you ain't heard in a while, or something totally out of whack, and if I was feeling a little playful then I'd slip it in. Then play the record.

It's good sometimes to keep your crowd expecting the unexpected. I see cats, DJ-ing. And they're going through the numbers. Playing the same songs at the same time. Like a guy I once knew of at Luciano's, Lower East side. I was there with some buddies of mine, one time. The place was heaving. And me and the boys were swinging in rhythm and catchin' a little girlie action, flirtation wise, with the odd mutual groping in passing.

'Hey Swanny, what time is it, man?'

'Oh, dunno man. Hey but is that Rod Stewart, 'D'Ya Think I'm Sexy'? Must be 11 0'clock, dude.' Replies Dan the man. You could set your watch by the playlist, as Dan will testify. When he's not spooning on the dance floor.

'Gracias, my amigo. Got hit the dirt. Gotta date with Big Sal.' And with that, Swanny swans off, me shaking my head in anguish. Everyone knew Big Sal was playing him for a chump. And playing the field, too. Heck, she'd rattled my bones one time with Dick behind her and Dan feeding her a hotdog sausage, whilst Swanny, the sap was opening up the Marabou for lunch.

He left the City not long after that night at Luciano's and I didn't see the cat for a while. Kinda missed him, 'n all, 'cos he was a friend and without your friends, y' aint got nothin'.

Saw him a few months down the line when he came in to the Paradise.

'Hey, Swanny. Me amigo, welcome to my casa. How's it hangin' dude and what's the scoop?' We jawed a bit while enjoying a white Russian.

Alexandra, her name was and she was auditioning as an exotic dancer over on the podium. She was grinding away with little tassels on and entreating me with half closed eyes and a come-to-bed flat stomach. I sighed and asked Swanny about Big Sal.

'Oh, she's not my girlfriend, no more, Rand.'

'Hot dang, Swanny.' I said. 'You is off the hook man, for sure! Man, that comes as a relief to me 'n the boys, I tell ya. That beast was dragging you down, dude. She just about laid everyone in Manhattan. A beauty, yes sir. And bouncy as anything, and I oughta know. And now I can let something off my chest and tell you I had me a fun old time playing around with *them* mighty big, love cushiony fun titties, hot jiminy. But I is overjoyed....'

And on I went, digging me a big ol' hole of no return. But enough about Big Sal.

'She's not my girlfriend, Randy. She's my wife.' He said, between gulps of indignation.

Looking back, I think I handled the twister quite well. I grabbed a hold of Swanny's hand, pumping away with bonhomie and told him what a remarkable lady he had. Practically showered him with congratulations, whilst simultaneously directing his gaze towards Alexandra as I topped up his glass with the right stuff, and she was bending over adjusting a stiletto. She even peaked around to enjoy us watching her tail. Dirty Desdemona.

A man has his weaknesses and that helped to soften the blow and release the tension. A close shave. Lucky I never told him about the gang bang. Alexandra played her part, too and I gave her the job over her left shoulder as me and Swanny made a Cossack sandwich on the stage. We was crossing swords and taking it in turns. At one point, we was even duelling, pistol on pistol. Thank God no-one got shot in the eye.

Afterwards we all hunkered down whilst Alexandra chopped out some white on her rock-hard belly for me 'n Swanny to go marching on our knees towards the Crimean valley. It was pure as snow, but with a gamey after taste.

Moral of the story is, if you are DJ-ing, don't take the easy option of pre-programming your entire evening. Or you'll be responsible for a whole heap of miscommunication and toying with another man's emotions. Its plum lazy, man, so mix it up. Upset the Status Quo, and I ain't talking 'bout the band. I'd never upset those guys, 'specially when they is hanging around your sitting room, eyeing up the coffee table.

Mama Feelgood loved those boys. In fact, she looked after them on one of their visits to the City in '68. Even wrote a song about her, *'Big Fat Mama'*. No offence was meant or taken and they used the bathroom instead of the furniture.

Big girls, you are beautiful. But play nicely.

GET DOWN – GENE CHANDLER

LE FREAK – CHIC

DON'T STOP TIL YOU GET ENOUGH – THE JACKSON FIVE

I'M EVERY WOMAN – CHAKA KHAN

HEART OF GLASS – BLONDIE

BOOGIE OOGIE OOGIE – A TASTE OF HONEY

IN THE BUSH – MUSIQUE

CONTACT – EDWIN STARR

SEPTEMBER – EARTH, WIND AND FIRE

DISCO NIGHTS (ROCK FREAK) – GQ

'78, what a year for the Disco sound. I could ha' included another ten tracks of red hot molten Disco records. And notice, there ain't no Soul in my selection. These are *my* top 10, remember and I'm bound by mah own rules, and kept on a leash. That's boogie bondage, right there.

Talkin' of which, I've included a track by my good friends, *Blondie*. A Punk band by rights, but this song is pure Disco, with the rhythm section tidied up and space-age synths. They'd gone a long way since I saw them with my punk pals.

Chapter 16

Keep the Customer Satisfied

Now, sometimes you need to use your mic to impart personal messages or information. Hell, and I encourage that personal one on one with my audience, less 'n they're buggin' me. Then I call over ol' Big Fat Bigfoot crappin' Eddie to hoof 'em out behind the bins at the back door.

Don't be jivin' me mister, or you'll be nestling down in a pile of horse manure and hobo piss. And this section kinda blends in and around what I'm talkin' about *talkin'*.

What I'm saying, is you have to use the mic wisely, and I always included the dancers, the crowd, the young and the old in mah show. Inclusivity, is the thing. But be careful, y'all. Ensure you got the message right.

One night I had this bunch of ladies in and one of 'em writes a little message for me to read out. I was a little distracted at the time as she was playing boob tennis with my hips at the time and I very nearly made a mess all over Diana Ross and into Gloria Gaynor.

"HIYA RANDY, CAN YOU SAY A HELLO TO ETHEL WHO'S Ill TODAY, THANKS RANDY. WE GIRLS THINK YOU'RE HOT STUFF". Well, I knew I had mass appeal. Whether it be black or white, straight or gay, young or old and I was still contemplating them soft ripe melons bulging out of that minx's blouse.

So, I made a big event o' reading out this touching birthday message, for a lady of considerable years. Admiring the fact that she was still swinging and dodgin' the coffin. After editing out the personal message for me, of course. That's when I realised what it actually said:

"HELLO TO ETHEL WHO'S ILL TODAY."

I blame the poor grammar, instead of poor grandma.

Woah, gotta make sure brothers and sisters, and not get taken in by the juicy fruit. Especially dancers from the Copa.

Talking of the older generation, I 'member my ol' grand pappy from England tellin' me 'bout the time he was in the trenches fighting for the Brits during the First World War, and the horror of the mud and the blood and the lice.

'What was it like Grand pappy?'

'Rained the first week', he replied as he puffed on his pipe, droppin' cinders all over his singed cardigan. 'We sent a message up the wire. "Send reinforcements, we're going to advance", but back at HQ, they transcribed it as "send three and fourpence, we're going to a dance."'

'Dang and tarnation,' you don't say Grandpa. I'd heard this old tale many times, but you get the point.

'Stupid buggers. But surprisingly, they actually did send the money. So, we thought we'd go to the dance after all. The band wasn't bad, despite bombs and shells going off every minute. No one to dance with except the widows from the village. And so, the following week, we asked 'em to "send three and fourpence" for the dancing again and the idiots sent over a picnic hamper and a dozen deckchairs, hee hee hee………' he was getting himself all excited now.

'Now calm down, ol' fella'. I said

'Nurse, it's happened again!' And then he glazed over as the memories started to fog and fade.

Requests are always to be welcomed. Keep a notebook next to ya, so as you can jot down what people is askin' for. Or get your

Man Friday, Bobby D to do it. He sure ain't doin' nothin' else, 'cept creating mood lighting, hitting the dry ice and neckin' all the beer.

But again, you gotta tread careful like. Keep the customer happy is what I'm tellin' you.

But I know what you're thinking:

'But Randy, it's your show man. You're the main dude, the soul brother number one, the sugar pimp daddy of the Disco dancefloor.' All true, of course. But I wouldn't be nuthin' without my adoring fans. I got the common touch see, as long as they don't touch without an invitation, you dig? Unless you're Brenda Castle or Big Sal, or Melody. Then I'll let it slide.

Therefore, sometimes you need a gatekeeper if people are getting a little over-excited or uppity. And when some cat comes up to ya, all sweaty and bleary, saying,

'Ah, yeah, hey man, my girlfriend wants you to play *'Yes sir I can Boogie'* by *Baccarra.*' Well I just about die inside. But you gotta keep your countenance, and maintain your poker face which is just on the cusp of contempt, but with a hint of condescension (which means looking down on someone).

'Hey man, cool choice, but ya know, I just got that very record out of its sleeve, and guess what. The damn thing's all scratched to hell and back, and won't play and on top o' that I think I may have chipped a nail. Now, how's about I play *'Got to give it up'* by Mr. Marvin Gaye, for your girlfriend and I promise she'll be tuned in, turned on and soul gone, yeah?'

All about the confidence to rectify a situation by taking control of that situation. Satisfaction guaranteed or take your love back, everyone's happy. Including *Baccarra*, who I used to invite to all my private soirees.

They later split up, as bands do. Not 'cos of my private parties you understand. Musical differences. But they both kept the band name. There was a time in the 'Eighties you could pay to go see two bands called *Baccarra*. Not me of course. I was always on the guest list.

Fads and fashions come and go, but the basics must remain. This is true, especially when it comes to your Club. It needs a dancefloor. That's your focal point and that's what your paying public want. I know entrepreneur types who have invested in some joint. They've painted it, installed state of the art, hi-tech equipment and then they go and stick the bar in a separate room to the dancefloor. What the heckety heck!

All the sisters are dancing in one room, and it's like a sausage factory in the other. All the guys are there, in their tight trousers. So tight, you can tell what religion they are, and they're hanging on to the bar like it's a life raft, tapping their rings against their pots and checking each other's hair and shirts.

At the same time, the broads are all dancing round their handbags and getting mighty lonesome for some male company. That's the problem when you let a suit own a place. Terrific hangout for me of course. I love to love, and I just love to dance so the 'Purple Alley' was right up my street. I was like the queen bee in that joint. Just doing the hustle as the chicks swarmed around me, whilst I feasted on their honey pots. Different times, baby.

You gotta have lights. Stage lights. Light it up, and create a mood. I played at one place, Barbarella's, in an old historical City called Southampton, England, where you remember Disco Dick once resided. You may even know the place.

It had lights actually inside the dancefloor. So, you was doing your dancing on a multi-coloured lit floor. That place was cool. Even had the DJ booth that went up to the second floor to the mezzanine bar area, then you go down to the main floor on first. It was a little mini elevator.

Made me a little dizzy, but that may have been down to the Champagne I was having with Bacardi and Bombay Sapphire at the time. Couple of beach volleyball players I was hanging with. A little crowded as the booth was only designed for one.

Baby, that place was rockin' as was the DJ Booth. Hell, I was up and the girls were going down, so we stopped in the middle during *'Ring My Bell'* 'til we got to the climax. Then I continued the journey south, where they could get off. Again.

Chapter 17

Pastime Paradise

In 1977 I acquired The Paradise Club, 254, West 53rd Street. It was an old derelict, abandoned theatre but the perfect size, shape and location for a nightclub. Me and Dick had bundles of cash, just then and needed to invest *toot suite* and this was the perfect spot.

We opened just about the same time as Studio 54 which was in West 54th Street, right around the back. Studio 54 was opened by two go-getters, Steve and Ian and the four of us had a combined vision of how we could best exploit all of our collective talents.

Both clubs had their back yards adjoining each other. You could walk through the Paradise, keep walking through the storage areas, through the back yard and right into the kitchen of 54. All secret of course. And there were also some security doors to negotiate as well.

We would often lend theatrical backdrops to Steve and Ian for some of the 54's wild parties. And it was a time I really got to know Nile and Bernard from *Chic*. I remember they couldn't get in to 54 one night and I happened to be strolling past the front door as I was coming out with Jane Fonda.

'Hey Nile, how ya doin' dawg?' I drawled and *one-potatoed* Jane.

'See ya later, Barbarella', I said, as she high-heeled it, giggling to a waiting cab. Maybe that was why that bar in Southampton was called Barbarella's? Could be.

I didn't really know Bernard that well, just then, but he seemed cool. And, well, you know we were two bass men, so we bonded over a G-string back at the Paradise.

Later of course, those two cats were never out of 54. In fact, Nile had a camp bed in the ladies' restroom. He spent his time lounging and powdering his nose. I felt sorry for the dude, despite the huge infectious gap-toothed grin he habitually wore.

There was a small outbuilding at the back of the Paradise, used mainly for storing soft furnishings and lampshades. I renovated this with the help of some of the girls and turned it into a small pad for the boys. I called it the 'Chic Boutique'. It allowed the boys a space for writing, relaxing and other activities.

Some magic was created in that little room, and I'd drop in from time to time just to sprinkle my own little magic dust, particularly on the backing singers. It's why their voices sounded so silky; I taught them some harmonising.

I had my balls in the air about that time. I was plate spinning, you know. You should try that some time and see how far it gets you.

Various business enterprises meant I couldn't run the Paradise myself. There just wasn't enough Randy to go around. So, I got me a guy I knew from the Gallery, a mostly gay club in the early '70s, name of Joyce Divine.

He was a big ol' girl from the Village who seemed to put his make up on with a paint gun from an Auto body shop. He always dressed in a tight-fitting sequined gown, usually sapphire blue. It accentuated all his curves, in all the wrong places. But he wore it with confidence, you know.

His assistant was a sullen Swedish chick of dubious gender, name of Svetlana Svensson. She wore the trousers, literally. It was a fitted pin stripe single breasted suit, with a flared leg and a white buttoned blouse. Her black hair was cut short and slicked back, which gave her a startlingly voluptuous appearance with dark eye shadow and bright red lipstick. But the most startling thing of all was her painted on moustache.

Together with her straining chest, she had me aroused on sight. There was no joy in those cold Scandinavian eyes, though, as they flickered around the place when the Club was rocking. And there was no joy when she seduced me next door at Bazooka's.

'Randy, I vaaant you,' she purred as I was testing the hot tub one evening. And she stripped down to nothing but her tight blouse and climbed in.

She didn't have much to do, in fact, as I was already halfway there, with the bubbles and all. I made a play for her wet shirt and found it all very erotic, massaging those Swedish boobies through the see-through fabric. It was all over in a tidal wave of splashing and grinding. Svetlana shuddered three times, then slid under the surface. I was getting worried at first that she may have swooned. I have that reputation. A full minute later she rose silently, without any ripples. like some kinda lady of the lake and climbed out.

'Saank you. It was very sexxxy pleasure for me,' she stated all matter-of-fact. Not once was there a glimmer of a smile, but it was different, that's for sure, and damn erotic. The water had cooled to the temperature of a cold bath and a chill was in the air. When I looked in the mirror, I had the impression of a moustache on my chest.

They made an odd couple Svetlana and Divine, as Joyce liked to be known. And I knew the Club was in safe hands with this Bonnie and Clyde at the helm.

'Til one night, when Joyce's doppelganger entered through the back door. This wasn't an entirely novel scenario. But this time it was like looking at twins. Granted, the most garish and horribly designed twins from some freakish Cinderella pantomime, with baubles and glitter smeared across sweat-streaked flabby chops in their creaking Christmassy dresses. The ugly sisters brought to the street.

This new interloper was the other, better known Divine. He'd heard about *my* Divine and wanted a showdown. Accordingly, he indignantly hitched up his ruby red sparkly frock over his water-retained bulging knees to clatter south through 54 on his man-sized stilettos. Out he pounded through the 54's kitchen, shaking the dumpsters, across both yards and in through the Paradise's open back door.

Dag nabbit! That dopey knuckle head crappin' Crump had left the door ajar, after carrying that blasted white stallion over his shoulders from its dressing room and into Studio 54's holding stable.

So, *54 Divine* was looking for *Paradise Divine* to claim the title of Drag Queen of New York City. In the red corner, Divine the Drag actor. In the blue, Joyce Divine from the Village.

Well, it all ended rather amicably, I thought. The two of them rolling around behind the bins, screeching at each other and tearing at clothes and throats with painted talons. Divine lost her wig, Joyce lost a fake boob, and the crowd who'd gathered to watch thought it a great hoot. Woody Allen thought it was all part of the entertainment, I recall, and even shouted 'encore' when it looked like it was winding down. It may have been ironic. But he was mightily beady eyed and somewhat enjoying the smell of testosterone and cheap perfume.

'My First Mistake' by the *Chi-lites* was leaking through the Paradise door and everyone was getting down to the vibe, punctuated by the grunts and baritone puffing and panting of the two lumbering cross-dressing hippos rolling around brawling in the

dirt. It was like watching any Friday night Honky Tonk bar bust up and was a memorable night.

Ultimately, both of them ran out of steam and Divine, the singer was declared the winner, and thus, the Alpha female. He went on to have a huge career and Joyce went back to being plain old Joyce, still in her dresses and war-paint and still keeping a tight rein on the Paradise. She could defuse a potential situation with just one look, while Svetlana would call the boys over to mop up any blood.

Last I heard she was living in Florida and goes out as a Divine tribute performer.

Ironic, man. Or woman.

Radio Randy 1979

DANCIN' IN OUTTA SPACE – ATMOSFEAR

STREETLIFE – THE CRUSADERS / RANDY CRAWFORD

LADIES NIGHT – KOOL AND THE GANG

WE ARE FAMILY – SISTER SLEDGE

FUNKYTOWN – LIPPS INC.

IT'S A DISCO NIGHT – THE ISLEY BROTHERS

GOOD TIMES – CHIC

HOT STUFF – DONNA SUMMER

I DON'T WANNA BE A FREAK – DYNASTY

SPACER – SHEILA B. DEVOTION

Hot dang diddly dang, but these platters are all that matters when it's Disco you're after. Again, I left out more 'n I put in. Somethin' I'm fond of saying to all my lady friends.

In my mind, this is when Disco hits its peak. Soul, as we know it, is out and Funk has had all the Funk taken out of it by Producers nodding over to the Studio Engineer, and sayin',

'Yo, cat, knock down the 'Bass' will ya and slide up the keyboards, there'. And that is a bottom disgrace. Soul has a resurgence in the 'Eighties, but that's another tale for another day.

An interesting point is that when Disco began, it had an association with all things spacey and silvery. Check out the video of *'Lady Marmalade'*, with the three chicks all in their sassy silvery figure-hugging spaceman outfits.

I did check them out one time and had a fine discussion on this very subject with Nona Hendryx. You know, the one with the sexy shaved head in the video. That chick's had lots of fantastical hairstyles over the years, but it's her saucy lower lip that gets me quivering all over, mmm hmm.

I guess, it was all due to space exploration and stuff with Apollos and rockets shooting off every other weekend, seemed like (the space themes, not the flirting and winking). Then we end up here, in '79 and we're top and tailed with spacey things. Which, incidentally is what happened to me with Patti Labelle and her gang.

Out of this world.

Chapter 18

Don't take away the Music

Remember I told y'all I'd lay it on you some fine tracks for mixing just to get ya started. So, this here's a little combo to get y'all worked up.

1.   Seesaw - Aretha

Get Ready - Temptations

Oye Como Va - Santana

Come See About Me - Junior Walker

You Keep Me Hangin' On - Supremes

A beat matchin' Soul segue which I recommend as an early night thang, just gettin' 'em warmed up. But when you feel like gettin' funky, but bringing the pace down, try these.

2.   Jungle Boogie - Kool and the Gang

Superstition - Stevie

Play That Funky Music - Wild Cherry

Rapper's Delight - Sugarhill Gang

Wicky Wacky - Fatback Band

Then you're back up to speed again, and ready to go in any direction.

3.   Got to Give It Up - Marvin

Le Freak - Chic

Higher Ground - Stevie

144

Get Up Offa That Thing - James Brown

Soulman - Sam & Dave

I Know You Got Soul - Bobby Byrd

Another transition moment, changing lanes and going up the gears.

4.   Funky Nassau - Beginning

Billy Jean - MJ

Get Down Saturday Night - Oliver Cheatham

Late in the Evening - Paul Simon

Soul Power '74 - Maceo

Bus Stop - Fatback

Superfreak - Rick James

1999 - Prince

Man, these snappers give you a taste of everything. Latin, Disco, Funk, Soul. And will guarantee the floor is on fire. Some '80s cuts there, sho' nuff but I'm giving y'all some mixin' ideas here and we'll get to the '80s in good time so don't drag me down.

5.   Love and Happiness - Al Green

Carwash - Rose Royce

He's the Greatest Dancer - Sister Sledge

Long Train Running - Doobies

It's a love train, Soul train kind of groove going on here.

Mixing, or beat-matching, or segueing as it was known at the start of the Disco revolution, was a vital tool to keep the dancers on the floor.

I've been to places where the sucker DJ 'll just stick a record on and let it play out before starting the next one. Candy ass dude got no Soul. And the people dancin', they is all just groovin' and getting' down 'til the volume starts fading and the momentum is gone. Like they is all powered up, maybe to impress someone they got their eye on. The motor is running and they're ready to burn some gas, and some rubber. Then you get that awkward moment (only lasts a second or two), when the engine is hot but the wheels are stopping, 'til the next record comes on and you can start bopping again. Uncomfortable. Like everyone is some kinda dancin' robot. The switch is flipped and everything shuts down and powers right back up again.

Now I am not digging that action, baby. And it's something I was aware of back in '73 when I was slidin' round the kitchen of the Shakin' Hand.

'This is a great song, and it has the same beat as this other great song, it's almost like I can hear both these great songs just coupling together'. I'd think to myself, going into a shagging daydream.

Now, sometimes it happened, (the mixing, not the other) but mostly it didn't. And when I returned to the big city late in '74 I strove to put these thoughts into action.

Nicky Siano was doing the same thing down at the Gallery. They had a similar crowd to us at the *Shakin' Hand* and then the *Catfish*. The oppressed minorities, I 'spose you'd call 'em; blacks, gays, Puerto Ricans, and cat ladies.

There was an underground scene, hidden from the cops who were down on anybody who stood for *anything* just then. They was tough times, with Nixon and the Vietnam War, Civil rights and anti-gay laws and all that jazz. And people just wanted to dance and party. Is that just too damn much to ask for? I don't think so. And neither did a lot of people. Except the authorities when my pal Skid Hazzard jumped ship in Vietnam and caught a container ship back to New York. But that's another story for another time.

We was creating what is now known, as modern club culture. Well, not Skid, obviously. He was tagging along for the ride. It really was revolutionary, in a Che Guevara kinda way, and there were berets and moustaches. But don't thank me just yet.

The drag queens certainly had a mini revolution in '69 when they stormed the police barricades after a bust at the Stonewall. Gay liberation for women, who are men, that's what I preach, preacher man. But I don't blame the cops from running away from a bunch of screeching Village girls in their high heels and beards. What would you do, faced with satin and lace, leather and chiffon and pumped up masculine pheromones all wrapped up in a six foot, four-inch frame tottering towards you on killer heels, handbag loaded? Heck, I'd have skedaddled, too. And I've seen Joyce Divine all fired up remember. Her face was enough to scare a shark.

Like I said, I do not run, unless I'm being chased. By a painted sappho daddy-o or lady man. Or a bunch of savage Indians, intent on you marrying one of their nieces. Or an angry husband, or Ma when she realises I've lent some big gay singer dude her best floral frock.

Up until the early 'Seventies, there was just private parties for like-minded and socially outcast ethnicities and sexualities. Hedonism and acid was the thing back then. Before my time, but I caught up real quick.

Then the *Gallery* opened which was the first openly gay club with state of the art lights and sound system and dry ice and glitter balls. And that place just swung.

And now some wise words of warning. There's a handful of tracks that should be treated with the utmost caution when you're doing you're mixing. And if you can't stand the heat, get out of the DJ Booth and into the kitchen.

'Stuck in the Middle', by Stealer's Wheel starts off all lightweight as the band nervously pick away at their guitars like they're frightened of Gerry Rafferty dropping a trouser bomb in the elevator. Then the groove kicks in and that's where you need to be starting the song, and avoid all the namby-pamby, wishy-washy guff.

'Lost in Music' starts on the off-beat. For intermediate DJ's only, 'cos if you get it wrong you're gonna look like Doofus McDork features.

There's other songs that you need to decide when you're gonna start the track, and more importantly, how you gonna end it. It's all fine and dandy showing off and doing your beat-matchin' and all. But comes a time when you'll wanna change lanes. Then you can crash a big hitter in. Say, '1999', or 'I Will Survive', or 'Somebody Else's Guy'. But you have to get the moment correctimundo or your brilliant piece of programming will fall flat, like a crappola tombola.

'Last Night a DJ Saved My Life' is another one to think carefully about. Great song with a thumpin' bassline. But d'ya wanna keep in the flushing restroom lavatory bit? How much? 'Away goes trouble down the drain'. But you can do a smart little manoeuvre here by slipping in another song with an instrumental intro. It's a small toilet window of opportunity. Try 'Carwash'. I know, I know, but we is talkin' advanced level plumbing, here.

Nicky Siano will regale you with his dream of having three turntables, with 'Love is the Message' by MFSB on one, the sound of a jet plane on another and who knows what else on the third. May as well have been a sound effect of some dork snoring, if you gonna play *'Love is the Message'*. That song is straight outta Snoozeville, Arizona.

He was probably dreaming at the same time as playin' the darn thing. With a Club full of people doing the dance of the zombies.

Programmin' your night is the same as romance. It's all about bringing the audience up, then down. Take it slowly, then be a little more forceful and slam in a whopper. Then toy with 'em a bit, before giving them a sideswipe and takin' them someplace new. Then you can lay back and fire up your pipe.

End of the night is the time to slow things down a little for the lovers out there. Two or three songs, just to get 'em panting then get those house lights up. Always leave 'em wantin' more. Depends on the crowd of course. They may be in the mood for a sing-a-long. Try Neil Diamond's *'Sweet Caroline'* or Olivia Newton John with *'Country Roads'*.

My absolute all-time favourite love song for romance, hope and positivity is *'Ain't no sunshine when she's gone'* from the sensational Bill Withers. Just think about the grammatical aspect of the lyric. *Ain't NO sunshine when she's gone.*

When she's around, there's no sunshine, probably due to the fact that she's a big ol' hefty beast of a woman. Maybe my Albanian monkey man, Mario's missus, or Betty, or Sal. She's blocking out all the light and the sun, with her thick fat head and stocky frame. Sad times, and all. But hang on. When she leaves, woah now. There's the sunshine and the prevailing air of gloom is lifted and all is bright and wonderful with the world.

'And I know it's gonna be, a lovely dayyyyyyyyyyyyyyyy'. Just like Bill Withers said, with one long breath and his face turning blue.

Now, I don't want to give the impression that beauty is only skin deep, no matter how much skin a lady has. Big can be beautiful, and I love curves as much as the next dude. Voluptuosity is invigorating and sometimes it comes to pass that the most outwardly beautiful woman with perfect shiny black shimmering hair, pearl white teeth set between slightly parted, full lips and model-like figure with coffee coloured skin can get on your nerves with their little ways.

Take Melody Crump, for example. Except, no. Please, don't take her. She was my own special lady. Always has been, ever since my eyes popped out at the sight of her dancin' at the Marabou one night. She was Eddie's little sister and they couldn't have been more different. She was twenty and athletic with sweet, ripe apples, a tiny waist and a dancer's legs. Supple, too. And Eddie, well he was a Buffalo trapped in a Rhino's body.

Melody had the sweetest face, framed with silky black hair, but she had a tiger in the tank. And I could just tell by a look that she wanted to wrap her long legs around me and play a marching tune on my lemon popsicle. Almost like she had little Melody muscles all playing a different tune on me, all singing harmonies of love, taking me to the edge and then back again. Juicy fruit sauce-pot. Mtume!

But as much as I was in love with Melody, and you know I go for the more mature type, me being nineteen at the time. Well, sometimes I just couldn't stand her little ways. Like asking me questions when I'm brushing my teeth.

Number one, I can't hear ya sugar, and two, I can't answer you with a mouth full of froth.

Empty milk cartons put back in the fridge, cupboard doors left open, and discarded lacy undergarments strewn throughout the bedroom. Just some of the things that she found tiresome about me, when she moved in temporarily.

But love will find a way, and we settled on an open relationship. I have got too much love for one woman. I got to share it out, and there's only so much Randy to go around. Melody was cool with that and understood the dilemma.

Besides, this was the '70's. A liberated age. And with artists such as Labelle and Donna Summer, women were throwing off the shackles of suffering and embracing freedom. Chicks were coming out of the kitchen and onto the dancefloor and shaking their booties. *More, more, more, how do you like it! Woah.*

New York had become more liberated. Similar to San Francisco where chicks could stand up and be counted. I do like a lady who knows what she wants and how to get it.

One of my favourite songs to play to start my nights, was 'Suffragette City'. I like to think David Bowie wrote that as a love letter to New York City. It has an energy and vibrant electricity just like the Apple itself.

Chapter 19

Let's Stay Together

It's the end of the night. The applause has dissipated into the night, carried by the breeze on gossamer wings and the erogenous human musky scent of ecstasy. And the sweat-drenched clothes and hair of hundreds of satisfied punters who've been dancin' all night.

The lights are up and you're contemplating a nice warm bed, and taking a well-earned sip from the brandy glass at your side. The lovers are still entwined on the dancefloor, still dancing to the song that faded away minutes ago.

The bar-hops and glass collectors are roaming the floor. They're taking their sweet time, 'cos they're looking for nickels and dimes and joints scattered amongst cigarette packets and discarded items of lingerie, particularly around the DJ Box, that have been dropped throughout the night.

There's a half-drunk Mojito on the bar again, her usual position. In danger of falling off and hitting her head on the barstool.

Disco Dick is still kicking out his platform soles and scatting away to a bunch of giggling Cheerleaders over by the ladies' restroom. That fat head Ed, the turd-smuggling monster is wrestling with a horse out back and Melody is gyrating gymnastically over on the podium. Lindy Bell is down to her black skimpies again and her petite booty is grinding away deliciously round the perimeter of the dancefloor, trying to attract Dick's attention. She certainly has mine!

Bingo Bongo Basil is swinging his dreads and doin' his own thang to some Lover's Reggae Rock I've just slipped on and he's drawing on a fat 'J'. And Joyce is mopping at his sweaty cheeks, mixing up the war-paint and resembling an artist's palette, that's been sat on by a chimpanzee. What a night, let's do it all again tomorrow.

Or the next night.

This book is dedicated to all of you who like to dance, and love music. To anyone that has been to a Disco, a Club, a party where there's a DJ, or not.

It's dedicated to anyone who loves the nightlife, who loves to boogie at the Disco, and Soul Funk brothers and sisters who live for the weekend, and partying.

If you dig music, this is for you. See y'around, brothers and sisters and go with it. But go Disco!

Acknowledgements

A huge thank you goes to my family, E, W and M, who have had to live with a guy with his head in the clouds during the construction of this book.

Thanks also to Greg Bennett for guidance and assistance, and giving me the confidence to write. Inspiration has dripped down from Del Storey, Rob Daly, Kathy Otto, Dirk Benedict, George MacDonald Fraser, George Carlin, Josh Feiner and music itself.

Thanks also to Tristan Pascoe and all at Orange Castle Publishing.

References

The Joy of Disco (2012) – Director Ben Whalley

Saturday Night Fever (1977) – Director John Badham

Shaft (1971) – Director Gordon Parks

Melody Makers (2013) – Director Pete Stanton

Q Rock Stars Encyclopedia – Dafydd Rees, Luke Crampton

Lonely Planet USA

British hit singles and albums – Managing Editor David Roberts

Dear boy, Keith Moon – Tony Fletcher

The Copa – Mickey Podell-Raber, Charles Pignone

Sweat Lodges – Julia Roller

David Soul: The life, the legend – David Tailford

This Ain't No Disco – Roman Kozak

About the Author

Blaze Hunter lives in Los Angeles with his four children, two dogs and a parrot, Melvyn and is married to Melody Crump.

He was the Specials editor for the New York Times from 1989 to 2001. He was asked to accept 'gardening leave' after being sick in a potted plant in the office. He is a prize-winning journalist and has written numerous self-help books, such as 'Cross-dressing for humans' and 'How to open toilet doors'.

He graduated from Harvard University in 1984 and received a master's degree from the London School of Journalism in 1986. He is Executive Chairman of the Seattle Sea Budgies soccer team for whom he played during the 1991/92 season.

When he is not writing, he enjoys walking his dogs, soccer statistics and window watching.

22026251R00088

Printed in Great Britain
by Amazon